Here's How I See

Here's How It Is

Other books
by Heather Henson

Dream of Night

That Book Woman
illustrated by David Small

Angel Coming
illustrated by Susan Gaber

Grumpy Grandpa
illustrated by Ross MacDonald

Here's
How I
See It

Here's
How
It Is

Heather Henson

Atheneum Books for Young Readers
New York   London   Toronto   Sydney

ATHENEUM BOOKS FOR YOUNG READERS

An imprint of Simon & Schuster Children's Publishing Division

1230 Avenue of the Americas, New York, New York 10020

For information about special discounts for bulk purchases, please contact Simon & Schuster Special Sales at 1-866-506-1949 or business@simonandschuster.com.

The Simon & Schuster Speakers Bureau can bring authors to your live event. For more information or to book an event, contact the Simon & Schuster Speakers Bureau at 1-866-248-3049 or visit our website at www.simonspeakers.com.

Also available in an Atheneum Books for Young Readers hardcover edition.

Book design by Mike Rosamilia

The text for this book is set in Bembo.

Manufactured in the United States of America

First Atheneum Books for Young Readers paperback edition May 2010

0310 OFF

10 9 8 7 6 5 4 3 2 1

The Library of Congress has cataloged the hardcover edition as follows:

Henson, Heather.

Here's how I see it—here's how it is / Heather Henson.—1st ed.

p. cm.

Summary: At almost-thirteen, Junebug has never felt right except as a stagehand at her father's summer theater, but after her parents separate and an irritating intern takes over her responsibilities, she discovers how hard life can be without a script to follow.

ISBN 978-1-4169-4901-5 (hc)

[1. Theater—Fiction. 2. Family problems—Fiction. 3. Actors and actresses—Fiction. 4. Asperger's syndrome—Fiction.] I. Title. II. Title: Here is how I see it; here is how it is.

PZ7.H39863Her 2009

[Fic]—dc22 2008022213

ISBN 978-1-4169-9773-3 (pbk)

ISBN 978-1-4391-6408-2 (eBook)

For my father and mother,
Eben and Charlotte,
(the roots)
and for my sister,
Holly
(the wings)

Here's
How I
See It
—
Here's
How
It Is

There's a theater for you. A curtain, two wings, and beyond that—open space.

—ANTON CHEKHOV, *The Seagull*

In a circle of light on the stage in the midst of darkness, you have the sensation of being entirely alone. . . . This is called solitude in public. . . . During a performance, before an audience of thousands, you can always enclose yourself in this circle, like a snail in its shell. . . . You can carry it with you wherever you go.

—CONSTANTIN STANISLAVSKI, *An Actor's Handbook*

after

I.

HERE'S HOW I SEE IT:

Everything is going to be okay, just like Dad said.

HERE'S HOW IT IS:

I don't know if anything will ever be okay again.

I gave my dad a heart attack.

I want to say it to the ambulance people when they rush through the door. But they just tell me where to stand so I will be out of the way while they lean over Dad and pump his chest and do mouth-to-mouth and lift him onto a stretcher.

I gave my dad a heart attack.

I want to say it to the guy who hovers over my dad

as we speed through town in the ambulance with the terrible siren wailing above us.

I gave my dad a heart attack.

I want to say it to the doctors when we burst into the ER, but a nurse takes me by the arm and pulls me the other way and gets me to answer questions about who I am and what grown-up she should call.

I gave my dad a heart attack.

I want to say it to Mom when she and Mama Duvall and Beck come running into the waiting room and Mom grabs me by the shoulders and peers into my face and says, "Junebug, tell me what happened!"

I gave my dad a heart attack.

I want to say it, but I can't.

before

the tempest

I.

HERE'S HOW I SEE IT:

I am an actress, and this is my big Broadway debut. The stage is silent, waiting. I step out from the wings and I am blind inside the light but I know the audience is out there, just beyond the glare. I can feel them. Hundreds of eyes, watching me.

I am breathing deeply, from the very center of my soul. I am waiting, waiting for the moment to speak my lines.

I am getting ready to fly.

HERE'S HOW IT IS:

I place my hands flat against the shimmering tin. Cool and smooth to the touch.

"Cue Thunder!" Coleman whispers, pointing a finger at me.

I take a deep breath and throw all my weight onto my thunder maker.

Crash!

Now I drum my fingers along the surface, the thunder rolling closer. I am not the first thing the audience *sees* onstage, but I am the first thing it *hears*.

Opening Night of the Blue Moon Playhouse! And we are starting with *The Tempest*. Nothing finer than the Bard, as Dad says. (That's Shakespeare.)

Dad also says there are no small parts, only small actors, and so even though I wish I was *onstage* instead of *backstage*, I make the most of my (very small) role as the *thunder* part of

A storm with thunder and lightning.

Now Coleman points to the group of MARINERS huddled in the wings, and they walk out onto the darkened stage. They are a motley crew, soon to be shipwrecked.

"Lights up!" Coleman whispers into the headset she wears, the one that connects backstage to the light and sound booth at the back of the house (that's the rows of seats where the audience sits).

Right on cue, the stage floods with light.

Coleman points to me again, and I really let loose. I am the drummer in a band. I am the storm itself.

Dad says acting is not really about *acting*, it's about *being*. Stella made fun of me in rehearsal, but when I'm rolling the thunder, I truly *am* the storm. I am aware of nothing else. I can't even hear the lines being spoken by the actors onstage.

Until the MARINERS let out a great yell all together.

Coleman taps once on my shoulder.

"Blackout!"

II.

HERE'S HOW I SEE IT:

I was destined to be an actress because I was born onstage.

My mother is a brilliant and famous costume designer, and on the day of my birth she was sewing frantically at the theater to finish the costumes before the Opening Night of a great Broadway show. When she felt the first pains she ignored them, because in the theater everybody knows that *the show must go on*! Plus she thought she'd have plenty of time.

She didn't.

I made my grand entrance center stage.

HERE'S HOW IT IS:

I wasn't actually born onstage, but I could've been.

"Late for your cue," Dad likes to say. "A major case of stage fright."

I was a whole ten days late in fact. It was hot. Mom was big as a house and grumpy to boot. She could hardly see the sewing machine over her enormous belly. (Mom *is* a brilliant costume designer, but she's not technically famous.) Even so, she was trying to finish up costumes for the Dress Rehearsal of the Play about the Scotsman (also known as *Macbeth*). But you're not actually supposed to say *Macbeth* aloud when you're performing it because there's supposed to be a curse on the play that goes all the way back to when it was first produced in the Bard's day and one of the actors died during a performance. (Actors are a really superstitious bunch.)

Anyway, when Mom first felt the pains, she did ignore them because she thought I still had stage fright. But then the pains got a whole lot worse and she realized I was serious about finally making my entrance. And so she waddled out to the car and drove herself to the hospital. (It's only a couple of miles.) She didn't want to bother Dad because he was right in the middle of Dress Rehearsal.

"I knew he wouldn't be any help anyway," Mom says. "He'd just be thinking about the play. And he's always hated the sight of blood."

Which is kind of funny when you stop to think about it because for his role as the Scotsman he ended up getting covered in the stuff. But of course onstage the blood is all fake.

III.

HERE'S HOW I SEE IT:

In my big Broadway debut I am the ingénue (that's the young female lead), and so I am always on the boards, as they say (that's the stage). There's never a moment's rest behind the scenes. I am always flying from one entrance to another, always rushing from the darkness of the wings into the warm glow of the stage lights.

HERE'S HOW IT IS:

After I've rolled thunder I slide down next to the mask flats (the fake walls that keep the audience from seeing what's going on backstage). It's "Lights up!" again, and a golden patch leaks along the floorboards, almost touching my toe. I hold my breath and listen, my sister's voice beginning the next scene.

Lucky duck.

Stella is sixteen (almost seventeen), which means she's old enough to snag ingénue roles.

O what I wouldn't give to be in my sister's place.

To be an ingénue, not just a sound effect.

To be MIRANDA to Dad's PROSPERO.

To be called "my cherubim" onstage and off.

My cherubim. (It's a cute angel.)

Stella stammers over a line. She misses a beat.

Opening Night jitters.

Silently I say the words with her. I know the part by

heart. It's from sitting in rehearsals hour after hour (like I've done practically my whole entire life), and it's from helping Stella run her lines (like I've done practically since I could read).

Shakespeare's words are kind of hard at first. (A lot of times I have no idea what they mean.) But once you get the rhythm, the sound is so beautiful, so graceful, it's like dancing.

I remember dancing once with Dad inside a spotlight. I was maybe four and he was dancing me around on his feet inside the light, everything warm and golden. Then Mom picked me up and whisked me out, into the dark. I began to wail right away, and I wouldn't stop until I was back inside the spotlight.

"A star is born," Dad said then, and there was laughter all around.

Now the laughter is outside my own head.

A good sign! Laughter already!

I can hear Stella's voice changing, becoming stronger, the audience giving her her stage legs, as Dad calls it, her confidence.

"'How came we ashore?'" MIRANDA/Stella asks.

"'By providence divine,'" PROSPERO/Dad answers.

These particular lines (MIRANDA is asking her father how they ended up on a deserted island) suddenly make me think of Mom, alone on her own distant shore (Mama Duvall's house smack in the middle of endless fields). I wonder what Mom is doing right this very minute while Dad and Stella and I are busy with Opening Night.

Is she sitting on the big wraparound porch? Is she staring out across the endless fields toward the Blue Moon?

Is she thinking about me?

Now I feel an ache, deep inside, the way it feels when the theater is dark, closed.

I shut my eyes and wish two things:

1. That Mom was here on Opening Night like always.
2. That the Blue Moon was never ever dark.

The first wish is "complicated," as Mom explained at the start of the summer when she packed up her clothes and her sewing machine and her rainbow bolts of cloth into the old truck and drove the three miles to Mama Duvall's house on the other side of the farm. (One side of the farm is a farm and one side is a theater.)

The second wish I've wished a hundred million

times in my (almost) thirteen years and it's never done any good. The Blue Moon is a summer stock theater, which means we're open only in the summer, and we do a different play every three weeks.

If Mom was here, everything would be just right.

If the Blue Moon never closed, I would never have to go back to (boring) school in the (boring) middle of nowhere, where everybody thinks *I'm* boring because I don't play sports (gag!) or do cheerleading (double gag!), because I'm not drop-dead gorgeous (like Stella) or cute and easygoing (like my brother Beck).

I'm just me.

JUNE OLIVIA CANTRELL (*aka JUNEBUG*), *twelve (almost thirteen) years old; future Broadway star.*

IV.

HERE'S HOW I SEE IT:

"Miss Cantrell, may I have your autograph?"

"Miss Cantrell, what a brilliant performance!"

"Miss Cantrell, you were destined to play this role!"

HERE'S HOW IT IS:

"Junebug, run and get me a glass of water, please."

"Junebug, we're out of tissues!"

"Junebug, could you get some ice?"

Gofer. That's actually the role I'm destined to play here at the Blue Moon (along with Thunder, of course).

"Junebug, I need some aspirin."

"Junebug, would it be terribly inconvenient to fetch me a cup of hot water with just a little honey and lemon?"

"Junebug, I forgot my dagger—hurry to the Prop Table and grab it for me, will you?"

The truth is, I don't really mind playing Gofer. At least all the gofering keeps me busy. I don't have time to dwell on the (tragic) fact that I never actually get to go onstage during *The Tempest*. And at least the actors act like I've hung the moon.

"Junebug, you're just a doll!"

"Junebug, you're the best!"

"Junebug, what in the world would I do without you?"

At least most of the actors act this way. My own sister is a different story.

"June*bug*, I stubbed my toe! I'm bleeding to death. I need a Band-Aid, like, *now*!"

Enter Stella. She always emphasizes the "bug" part like I am something to be squashed. And she is always in need of something "like, now."

STELLA ROSE CANTRELL, *beautiful but vain; played the Nice Sister once upon a time; now plays the Mean Sister to perfection; rolls her eyes a lot.*

"Your Band-Aid, milady." I give a dramatic bow once I've gofered my sister's request, awaiting the proper gratitude, but (of course) none comes. Stella is too busy staring at herself in the dressing room mirror. (This is her favorite pastime when not onstage.)

"'Alas, alack,'" I mumble to myself, turning away from my ungrateful wretch of a sister.

"Alas, alack" is how you complain in Shakespeare. It's how all the actors talk, since they've been rehearsing *The Tempest* for three weeks. When they're sad, they sprinkle their sentences with words like:

> Alas, alack!
> O, my heart bleeds!
> O, woe the day!

And when they're happy, they say things like:

> O, wonder!
> O, a cherubim!
> Cheerly, cheerly!

Back in the wings I stand and watch the rest of the play. The actors flutter past as they make their Entrances and Exits. Some grin and wave at me or make funny faces; others stay in character, waiting for their cues.

The air around the stage is charged, staticky—the way it feels during a sudden summer thunderstorm. Purely electric.

"Nothing like Opening Night!" Dad will say. "A bit of terror mixed in with the excitement! Is everything ready? Will it all turn out right or will it be a complete and utter disaster? Will we please the Theater Gods or anger them?"

And tonight we seem to please the theater gods because there are none of the terrible mistakes or accidents that can sometimes plague an Opening Night.

No missed cues. (Like when an actor is late for an entrance.)

No long, painful pauses. (Like when an actor is late for an entrance and the actors onstage have to try to pretend like nothing is wrong.)

No unscheduled blackouts. (Like when the light and sound guys accidentally dim the lights early.)

No botched sound effects. (Like Thunder rolling too early or too late.)

"When the Theater Gods are pleased," Dad will say, "there's nothing like Opening Night! Nothing like it in the whole world!"

And it's true. Not even birthdays are better than this. Not even Christmas.

And just like birthdays and Christmas, it's over before you know it.

"Blackout!" Coleman murmurs into her headset after PROSPERO/Dad has given his final speech. (In Shakespeare, there always seems to be a final speech, kind of summing things up.) "Cue sound!"

Obediently the lights go out. The music swells.

It's "Lights up!" once more, and the actors bound back onto the stage, smiling and lining up to take their bows. The audience applauds—a wonderful sound!

Nothing like applause, either.

From the wings I close my eyes and imagine Dad beckoning to me.

"We can't forget Thunder!" his voice booms. "Thunder must take a bow! What would the play be without our dear, sweet Thunder?"

Of course I must be coaxed onto the stage because I'm so very modest.

"Go ahead, take a bow, Junebug!" Dad whispers into my ear. "You deserve it!"

And so I do. I bow.

Immediately the audience rises from their seats, clapping wildly, cheering and whistling and stomping their feet.

"A Standing Ovation!" Dad cries, gazing down at me, green eyes twinkling with pride, with love. "All for you, my cherubim!"

"June*bug*! Earth to the bug brain."

Enter Stella again.

"I am not a bug brain," I reply, glancing around to see if any of the other actors exiting Curtain Call are catching this scene. Stella has a wonderful habit of embarrassing me in front of an audience.

"Well, you were in total la-la land. Who knows what goes on in that bug brain of yours?"

She shoves one of her Props at me before rushing back to the dressing room to make sure she's still beautiful.

Prop Mistress. Yet another (behind the scenes) role I was destined to play.

Small, yes, but important.

After all, it is my responsibility as Prop Mistress to gather up the Props the actors use during the show and make sure they're safely back in their rightful place on the Prop Table so that they'll be ready and waiting for tomorrow night's show.

Most of the Props for *The Tempest* are old-time weapons—daggers, swords (fake, of course). And so I'm armed to the teeth when I nearly collide with a body lurking in the shadows.

"Oh, sorry!" I cry, managing to hold on to my armful of weapons while at the same time giving the body a quick up and down.

Enter a stranger.

BOY, *about my age; a little taller; light brown hair.*

"Can I help you?" I ask, assuming the boy is an

audience member, come to check out the backstage after the show. Maybe even get an autograph.

No response. None whatsoever.

"Are you looking for someone?" I try.

Still the boy doesn't answer. He seems completely oblivious to everything around him (even me), eyes gazing upward, intently studying something over-head.

"D-did you know that in Shakespeare's t-time the roof over the stage was c-called the heavens?" he asks.

Now I gaze upward too. A slanting roof with cross-beams to hold the various stage lights. The roof doesn't extend beyond the stage. When the audience looks up, all they see is sky.

"Theater under the stars!" Dad likes to say. The Blue Moon is not only a summer stock theater, it's an outdoor theater as well. Just like way back in Greek times or during Shakespeare's day.

I know all about the heavens. (I was *practically* born on the stage after all!) If I were Dad, I'd be able to quote something from Shakespeare at this very moment, a perfect reference to the heavens. But I can't. I can recite lines from plays we're doing during the summer, but I don't have Dad's amazing memory for every play Shakespeare ever wrote.

"And the space b-below the stage was c-c-called . . ."

I wait for the boy to say the word that rhymes with "fell," but his voice simply trails off.

"Yeah, I know. But we don't have the space below," I inform him. "Our stage is concrete."

Now the boy's gaze shifts to the floor. I'll admit we did a great job painting the concrete in overlapping shades of green to create the overall effect of a lush island paradise, but it's not like the painted concrete is the most fascinating thing in the world.

"Are you looking for your parents?" I ask. The weapons in my arms aren't heavy, but they're awkward. "Maybe your folks are at the party already? The party's not back here. It's in the rehearsal room—past the patio." I point a sword up past the last row of seats.

Opening Night party. First night of each new show. During which the actors mingle with the patrons and they all eat, drink, and be merry (which means everybody acts silly).

"D-d-do you need help with those?" The boy is staring at the sword now.

I give a firm shake of the head. Nobody touches the Props during the run of a show. Except the Prop Mistress (me). And the actors, of course.

"No thanks." I turn and head for the Prop Table, which sits behind the stage left entrance.

The Prop Table is actually two long rectangular tables pulled together and covered completely with sheets of plain brown butcher paper. Over the past couple of days I carefully traced and labeled each and every Prop from the show with a large black Magic Marker. (This is something I learned years ago by observing Prop Mistresses and Masters of seasons gone by.)

"C-c-cool."

The boy has followed me. In fact he's standing so close, our arms almost touch. I assume he's talking about the pile of weapons I've just deposited and am now sorting through. All the guys my age around here love weapons. At school they talk endlessly about guns or they draw pictures of guns and tell stories about going hunting with their dads or granddads.

I hate guns, even though my own grandmother owns one. But Mama Duvall doesn't hunt. She only keeps a rifle for rascally critters, as she says. She hates moles the most. Moles can tunnel through miles and miles of earth, making the fields squishy and useless. Whenever she catches sight of one coming up for air, she runs for her shotgun and takes aim. She's a pretty good shot.

"D-d-did you make this P-Prop Table yourself?" the boy asks, running his hand along the butcher paper instead of the swords and daggers.

I nod, surprised he even knows what a Prop Table is.

"What else d-d-do you do?"

The stutter is a soft flutter like butterfly wings, barely there.

I open my mouth but no words come out. There are so many duties at the Blue Moon, especially since Mom left. I don't know where to begin. And who is this kid anyway? Why does he want to know?

"I roll Thunder," I answer finally, thinking this will throw him.

The boy's chin comes up and he looks at me— really looks at me—for the first time in our brief scene together. His face is long and thin, and his dark eyes are nearly covered by a curtain of lightish brown hair.

"I liked the Thunder," he says, eyes sweeping down

again. "It was very . . ." He seems to have trouble making his lips form the word. "B–b–believable."

"Trace? Trace, honey, come meet Mr. Cantrell."

A voice, twangy like a country song, calls out of the dark behind us. I glance sideways at the boy—the call must be for him—but he doesn't react. He's studying the Prop Table like he's studying for a test.

"Trace!" A nervous laugh, and then impatience. "Trace Weaver, come here this second! I'd like you to meet Mr. Cantrell."

Now the boy turns, without a word to me, and follows the voice, disappearing around one of the mask flats.

"There you are!" Another nervous laugh. "This is my son. This is Trace. Trace, honey, this is Mr. Cantrell! He owns this place! He was in the play too, remember?"

"Hello, young man," Dad booms, still in his stage voice.

I tiptoe toward the voices and peer through a tiny gap in the mask flats so I won't be seen.

A skinny woman in tight jeans and tank top, teased-up blondish hair, is gripping the boy against her with one skinny arm like she's afraid he'll disappear.

"Did you enjoy the show, young man?" Dad grins and cocks his head to one side, waiting for the usual gushing response from an adoring fan.

"N-n-nobody really knows exactly how Shakespeare's p-plays were p-performed in his day. There's only speculation."

A pause. And then Dad leans back and lets out a great roar of a laugh. It's his stage laugh. His real laugh isn't quite so loud.

"Ah, yes, that's right!" Dad cries. "I can see you know something about the Bard, young man."

Immediately there's a strange tightness in my chest.

"Oh, Trace is just crazy about that stuff! He knows all about theater." The word is drawn out into three syllables. Thee-ate-ter. "He knows all kinds of weird stuff nobody else cares about."

"Well, that's just terrific!" Dad is gazing at the boy with the same kind of intense look he gets when he's directing a play and a scene isn't quite working yet. "You must be very proud of him."

"Don't know what to do with him, more like."

"Hmmmm." Dad tugs thoughtfully at the (fake) beard attached to his chin. And then he whirls abruptly about, his colorful PROSPERO cloak billowing dramatically out behind him.

The mom glances down at her son, obviously confused. I'm used to Dad's quick exits, of course, his sudden bursts of speed, but it takes a while for most people.

Roadrunner.

That's what Beck named him long ago (after that old cartoon), because Dad's always rushing from one thing to another, faster and faster and faster, so that when he's at full speed you almost don't see his legs moving anymore. Summertime is prime Roadrunner season because Dad is always on the go, directing, acting, building sets.

"Plenty of time to rest in the grave," Dad will say when people marvel over his speed.

Now Dad must realize his guests haven't followed. He turns and beckons. "Won't you come this way?" He gestures grandly toward the Dressing Rooms. "We can talk in here."

The mom hesitates a moment, long enough for the boy to peer back into the shadows, right where I'm standing. I slide sideways, even though I'm sure he can't actually see me through the crack in the flats.

"We'll enjoy having your son here with us!" I hear Dad say. "He'll be a wonderful addition to our company."

Here with us? Wonderful addition to our company?

What in the world is Dad talking about? The boy is definitely around my age. Way too young to be an apprentice. Apprentices come to study theater. They do all the tech work, and sometimes get to do a little acting, too, if they're lucky. The apprentices are at least eighteen and in college already.

"I'm just glad we found you!" I hear the woman gush before their voices fade.

I stand perfectly still, trying to work it all out, the scene I've just witnessed, and then I hurry toward the Dressing Rooms so I can get to the bottom of this mystery. But I am stopped dead in my tracks, blocked, cornered, by a huge beast who roars and thrashes his arms into the air.

"'O brave monster!'" I cry out, shielding my face with my hands, because it is CALIBAN, who has the body of a man but the head of a beast. "'Alack for mercy!'"

In *The Tempest*, CALIBAN is the rightful king of the deserted island, but he is lazy and obstinate, moody and fierce, and not very bright. In the play, PROSPERO has tricked him out of a cloak of magic to become the king of the isle himself and has made CALIBAN his slave.

Now CALIBAN has stopped his roaring. In fact, he's kind of whimpering. So I reach up and give the beast a pat on the head. He leans down to gently nuzzle my hair with his donkeylike nose. I give a little scratch between his long, donkeylike ears.

"Will you help me get this thing off, Junebug? It's a bit tight. . . ." The voice is muffled inside the mask.

I take a firm hold, both hands around the neck of the beast, and pull.

Enter Ray, the actor who plays the monster.

RAY MONDELLO, *character actor; round and jolly; a "hail-fellow-well-met" (that's Shakespeare for "cool dude").*

"Ah, that's better!" Ray takes a deep breath after his head has been removed. "Methinks the beastie will be the death of me. It's pretty hot inside there, once you get under the lights. I may just pass out one night." He hands the thing over and pulls a bandanna from his pocket to wipe his sweat-streaked face. "I hate to tell you, but he's shedding some, and then I accidentally bumped into a tree out there during Act II. The nose is dinged, I'm afraid."

"Methinks I can fix him up good as new," I reply, cradling the fuzzy thing in my arms. The beastie is sort of a cross between a donkey and a bear head. Mom made it out of chicken wire and papier-mâché and fake fur before she left. Now I'm supposed to care for the beastie, like some poor abandoned pet.

"You're just a peach, Junebug," Ray says in a high-pitched, old lady voice. (He's always breaking into different accents like a lot of actors do.) He reaches out to pinch my cheeks. "A good show, methinks? What say you, dollface?"

"Good show," I quickly reply. I haven't known Ray very long (the actors have only been here for three weeks) but I love how he seems to really care about my opinion.

"See you at the party then, honey pie? Save a dance for me?" Now the accent is deeply Southern.

I nod my head.

"Anon!" he calls over his shoulder as he exits the scene.

"Anon," I call back. (Shakespeare for "later.")

With the beastie under my arm, I continue on toward the Dressing Rooms, but I don't hear the twangy voice anymore. I do hear a few of the ladies still primping in the Ladies' Dressing Room for the party, but when I knock on the Men's Dressing Room, it's only Dad. He's sitting alone in front of the long mirror.

CASSIUS HARLAN CANTRELL, *older leading man; longish, dark hair with a few streaks of gray flowing from the temples; not only acts, but directs; the esteemed founder of the Blue Moon Playhouse.*

"How now, daughter?" Dad's voice echoes in the empty room. He has taken off the fake beard, but he is still PROSPERO. I know it takes a while to shake a character after a show.

"How now, Daddy-O?" I respond with the usual and plop down in the chair beside him. "Who's the kid?" I decide to cut to the chase.

"Kid?"

PROSPERO looks totally confused.

"The boy you were talking to after the show."

PROSPERO transforms into Dad at last.

"Oh, you mean . . . let's see, what was it . . . Trace Weaver?"

A nod of the head.

"Didn't I tell you?"

A shake of the head. And a sigh. (Alas, alack.) Nope, didn't tell me.

"They're new in town," Dad continues. "The mother wondered if we could take any interns. Apparently the boy is quite the young thespian."

Quite the young thespian?

"B–b–b–but we don't have interns!" Who's stuttering now?

"Well, I thought it wouldn't cause any harm. We can always use an extra pair of hands around here. Especially this summer. And besides, it'll be good for you. Someone your own age about for a change."

My mouth drops open. I could catch flies (as Mama Duvall says).

I don't really like kids my own age. Never have.

I've lived my whole entire twelve (almost thirteen) years in this same small town, where everybody knows everybody else. I should have plenty of friends.

But I don't.

All summer long I'm surrounded by actors and

directors—grown-ups who think I'm this funny, precocious, mature-for-my-age kid.

But when the summer ends, when the Blue Moon darkens and empties, I'm like Cinderella at midnight. *Poof!* I return to being June*bug*, the squashable little sister of Stella (who seems to fit in no matter where she is) and Beck (who doesn't seem to care if he fits in or not, so he fits in anyway).

Mom says I don't try hard enough to fit in, but why should I, when the kids around here just look at me like I'm an alien?

The thing is, I know exactly who I am in the summer, what role I'm supposed to play. But for the rest of the year—when the actors have left, when the Blue Moon is empty, when I'm back in school—it's like I've lost the script, forgotten the lines.

Dad knows all this. He's held my hand when I've come down with sudden "stomachaches" because I dread going to school to face the humiliation of being weird. He's quoted beautiful words to me to make it better (he can always quote something that fits). We've talked about how he often felt the same way when he was a kid—like he was from another planet.

But now he seems to have forgotten. He's totally oblivious to my flycatcher face as he rubs cold cream in broad circles along his cheeks. I watch in silence as PROSPERO melts off onto wads of Kleenex.

"Does your dad really wear makeup and dresses sometimes?" Billy Cooper asked me on the playground in first grade.

"Yes," I answered proudly.

"Well, then he's a weirdo!" Billy Cooper yelled.

I was a flycatcher then, too. It had never occurred to me that other dads didn't put on makeup and costumes now and then.

"Your dad's a weirdo!" Billy Cooper repeated, and then he ran around the playground yelling, "Weirdo! Weirdo!" and telling everybody my dad wore makeup and dresses like a girl, and everybody stared and whispered for the rest of the day, for the rest of the year.

For the rest of my life.

"Dad?" I ask now.

"Mmmm?"

O where to begin? O so many things to ask!

Like why he thinks we need another kid here at

- 33 -

the Blue Moon when there's never been another kid (except me).

Like why everything is different this summer.

Like why Mom left.

"Dad," I start again, determined to reach him.

"Mmmm?"

But it's like he's a million miles away.

I get that same ache I got before, when thinking about Mom on the other side of the farm.

Mom is three miles away, but Dad is truly here, three inches away, and still it's like he's on his very own "distant shore." And I don't know why.

The thing is, Dad and I used to talk about *everything*.

Like what it means to want to be a serious actor.

Like what it feels like to actually walk onto a Broadway stage—even if it's only once in your life.

Like why it's important to do Real Theater (Shakespeare and other serious plays) at the Blue Moon, when a lot of people don't really appreciate Real Theater around here (the middle of nowhere).

But this summer everything is different. This summer Dad isn't talking about much of anything. At least not to me.

"Cass, are you ready?"

A voice floats around the corner and I know any chance to ask Dad my questions has vanished. *Poof.*

"I hope you're ready, goodly sir, because I want to dance the night away!"

Enter Lelia, and *O, my heart bleeds!*

LELIA DURNBOW, *leading lady; tall and slim; curly dark hair with creamy skin; in a word: stunning.*

In *The Tempest*, Lelia plays ARIEL, *an airy spirit,* who serves PROSPERO and plays tricks on his enemies. The thing is, ARIEL is usually played by a man, but Dad (as Director) turned the role into a woman and gave it to Lelia.

"'A fine apparition,'" PROSPERO/Dad calls her, onstage and off. "'My quaint Ariel.'"

I get a knot in my stomach just thinking about it.

Mom said I was too young to understand everything, the reason for the summer split, but I'm not completely clueless. I know Lelia is a big reason why Mom left.

"Oh, hi there, Junebug!" Lelia coos when she realizes Dad is not alone. "Getting ready for the party?"

I shrug.

"I hope you're not planning to wear the beastie to the party?" Lelia asks, laughing a little.

I glance down at the mass of fur on my lap. I'd forgotten I was still holding him.

"Wouldn't want to hide that pretty face of yours!" Lelia adds.

I give a little smirk, but it doesn't matter. Lelia is looking at Dad.

And he's looking back. A blank, lost look like when an actor forgets his lines onstage. It's a totally new expression for Dad. I've never seen him forget his lines onstage.

"'Go thither, Spirit!'" Dad murmurs, his voice turning smooth like velvet, the way it always does when he quotes Shakespeare.

Usually I love to hear him "speak the speech" as Shakespeare says in some play, "trippingly on the tongue." Now it only annoys me.

"Enjoy the 'marvelous sweet music,' my chick," he says. (Chick is another thing PROSPERO calls ARIEL onstage because he/she is supposed to fly like a bird.) "I'll be there anon."

"Yes, noble master, anon." Lelia gives the same kind

of bow she does as ARIEL and turns to leave. "Great show!" she chirps before she exits.

"*Great* show?"

Dad doesn't seem to notice my perfect imitation of Lelia's chirp.

"Not a bad show," he replies after a thoughtful moment.

"But not humming, right?"

Dad's best compliment. When something is really working, it hums.

"Definitely not humming. Not yet."

I wait for Dad to say something about my thunder rolling. Good or bad. Humming or not.

"Methinks I'm in need of a quick shower before the festivities." Dad rises and places a hand on my head—briefly—before turning for the door. "Anon, my pet."

"Anon," I mumble, but I don't make a move. Not yet. I sit perfectly still, gazing down at the mass of fur in my arms, and then I duck my head and pull the beastie on.

It's awkward and heavy at first. The head bobbles back and forth, my shoulders adjust to the weight. Inside the mask it's a strong mix of makeup and sweat.

You'd think I'd be grossed out, but I'm not. Somehow the smell—so familiar!—makes the knot in my stomach loosen.

"Quite the young thespian!" I quietly mimic Dad's velvety stage voice. Inside the beastie my words echo, deep and grand. "I declare that henceforth he shall be called Thespis, first actor of ancient Greece."

I sit staring at myself in the mirror—half beast, half girl—and let out a low growl. I have a feeling my life is about to change—again!—and I don't like it. Not one little bit.

V.

HERE'S HOW I SEE IT:

I was destined to be an actress not only because I was born onstage, but because I come from a long line of actors harking back to the beginning of theater itself.

In ancient Greece we were thespians performing in masks for gods and mortals alike.

In the Middle Ages we were traveling vagabonds

roving the countryside (the first touring company!), making music and drama for rowdy commoners and rich dukes and duchesses, regal kings and queens.

Rumor has it we were on the boards when Shakespeare staged his first play (even if it's not known exactly how it was staged).

And when it was time to cross the Atlantic we were there, on the ship, ready to bring theater to the New World.

We made our entrances and exits on a street called Broadway long before it became *the* Broadway.

And so acting is in my blood.

HERE'S HOW IT IS:

Dirt and manure, courtroom dust. That's what's really in my blood.

I come from a long line of farmers (on Mom's side) and a long line of lawyers (on Dad's side).

Stable. Practical. No nonsense.

Nobody on either side had ever entertained the far-fetched notion of going onstage.

Until Dad.

"I'd always acted in school plays," Dad has told

me. "And I'd go to the movies and just sit through the matinees all afternoon, watching those actors on the big screen. But college—that's when I really got bit by the theater bug. One drama class and that was that. There was no going back."

Of course Dad did go back. He came home (to the middle of nowhere) after college and he explained to his parents that he wanted to go to New York City to become an actor instead of going to law school to become a lawyer.

Of course the news didn't go over so well.

"An actor?" Grandpa Cantrell yelled. "What put that crazy idea into your head?"

Dad tried to explain, but Grandpa Cantrell wouldn't listen. He was too busy yelling.

The thing is, Grandpa Cantrell had had Dad's life all planned out since before Dad was even born.

CASSIUS HARLAN CANTRELL JR.'S LIFE

WRITTEN BY CASSIUS HARLAN CANTRELL SR.

ACT I

Attend same college all

here's how i see it — here's how it is

(male) Cantrells attend.

ACT II

Attend same law school all

(male) Cantrells attend.

ACT III

Return home and work

in the same law firm with all

the other (male) Cantrells.

Dad had a different play in mind, though.

CASSIUS HARLAN CANTRELL JR.'S LIFE

WRITTEN BY CASSIUS HARLAN CANTRELL JR.

ACT I

Catch the first bus to New York City.

ACT II

Find a place to live and a job. (Actually,

a lot of jobs, including dishwasher, taxi

driver, moving guy, waiter.)

Act III

Study with some of the best

acting teachers in the world.

Act IV

Become a serious actor and get

a role in a big Broadway show.

Dad's version of his own life actually got produced. After studying for years in the big city, going to every audition, he even got a teeny tiny part in a brand-new Broadway play. But when he called to tell his parents the great news and to invite them to come to New York City for his big Opening Night, his mom was crying.

Cassius Harlan Cantrell Sr. had had a heart attack.

Dad went onstage that one night (*the show must go on!*) and flew home the next day. But he was too late. Grandpa Cantrell was gone.

And so Dad gave up his teeny role on Broadway and stayed on to help his mom sort out all the loose ends at the law firm and transfer it over to the partners. He still intended to go back to New York City when things were settled, but then he met my mom.

The way Mom and Dad used to tell the story (when they used to live in the same house), it was love at first sight (like Romeo and Juliet). Their eyes met across a crowded room (the Dairy Dip on a summer night). It was a whirlwind romance (a whole month) and then they were married and lived happily ever after (until now).

At first Dad planned to take Mom back to New York City, but then they had Becket (named for one of my dad's favorite playwrights). Then Stella (named for a character in one of Dad's favorite plays) came along.

By the time I was born (named only for the month I was *supposed* to have been born in), Mom and Dad weren't talking about going back to the big city. Dad had already started the Blue Moon.

VI.

HERE'S HOW I SEE IT:

The new intern (aka Thespis) gets a major case of stage fright. On the morning of his big Blue Moon debut, he is paralyzed with fear and can't even leave his bed. He tells his mom that he's made a huge mistake. He can't possibly go among so many strangers. He doesn't want to be an intern after all. In fact, he's decided to give up theater altogether.

HERE'S HOW IT IS:

Thespis is already at the Blue Moon when I arrive early the next morning for Breakfast Duty. He's standing on the patio outside the kitchen, gazing upward yet again.

"No heavens up there," I inform him. "Just plain old roof."

I wait for a response, or even a proper greeting, but none comes. I'm about to turn away—how rude this boy is!—when a voice stops me.

"Oh, hey there!"

The same country twang from the night before.

Enter Thespis's mom, from the Ladies' restroom.

THESPIS's MOM, *bone thin; dressed as before in tight jeans and a tank top that reveals wiry but muscular arms.*

"Are you Mr. Cantrell's little girl?"

I'm about to object to being called a "little girl," but the mom doesn't wait for an answer.

"Junebug, right? That's just so *cuuute*! I had a cousin we used to call Junebug. But that's because she was always rushing around from one thing to another. Never could sit still from the time she could crawl. And she was just as noisy as a June bug in July too—never stopped buzzing on about any little old thing."

"June bugs are actually a type of b-b-beetle," Thespis says. His gaze sweeps over me and lands on the floor.

The mom gives me a look like the two of us are in on some secret together.

"This boy of mine!" She shakes her head in mock disbelief. "He packs a whole lot of information inside that brain of his."

Without warning she turns and throws her arms around Thespis, pulling him tightly to her (fairly substantial) bosom. An alarmingly aggressive hug, if you ask me. I expect the boy to pull away, like most boys would do, embarrassed. But the weird thing is, Thespis doesn't move. He doesn't seem to react at all. It reminds me of a National Geographic show I saw once on grizzly bears. The narrator explained how you're supposed to just go limp and still when bears attack.

"Now, Junebug!"

The mom releases Thespis and turns to me again. I shrink back a little, afraid she's going to try the grizzly bear hug on me. Luckily she keeps her distance.

"Mr. Cantrell said to get here first thing. And he said you'd show my boy the ropes, Junebug. You two are the same age, I guess, which is just so perfect. You're twelve, right, honey?"

"I'm almost thirteen," I announce, trying to sound older and stand taller. (I'm short for my age.) But it doesn't make any difference. The mom doesn't notice.

A country tune, vaguely familiar, has started blaring out of nowhere. There's a frantic search through the massive bag slung over one shoulder until finally the cell phone is located and flipped open.

"Yeah, yeah, I'll be there in a minute!" the mom says into the phone, without even a hello, and immediately flips it shut.

Now she gives me a superwide grin and takes a step forward. I flinch, telling myself to remain still, whatever happens, but she only reaches out and rests a hand on my shoulder, leaning down to my level.

"Junebug, honey, your daddy told you about Trace, didn't he?" She's still grinning, but her brown eyes are searching my face, waiting.

"Sure," I reply, resisting the urge to roll my eyes à la Stella.

Quite the young thespian.

La-di-da.

"Great!" She gives my shoulder a tight squeeze. "Well, I've got to get to work. Nice to meet you, Junebug. Take good care of my guy, now, okay?"

She doesn't wait for a reply, but turns and envelops Thespis in yet another fierce embrace.

"You be good, Trace, okay?" Her face is so close to his their noses are almost touching. "You do what Mr. Cantrell says." A pause. "You hear?"

A bob of the head, barely noticeable, but the mom seems satisfied. She turns and exits the scene, the sound of the country song starting up again and her voice, fading, but full of annoyance, "I said I'm on my way!"

In a play, when a particularly vivid character exits the stage, the actors should always wait a beat, give the audience a chance to digest what they've just witnessed.

That's what Dad always says when he's directing. And so that's what I do now.

I stand perfectly still, waiting for the mom's energy (and her perfume) to fade. But I'm also waiting for Thespis to say something about what just happened.

Most kids I know would make some crack about how wacky their mom is.

"D-d-did you know that Aristotle is the father of dramatic theory?" Thespis says instead, eyes still on the floor.

"Huh?"

"Aristotle b-believed that a play is an imitation of an action and not the action itself."

"Um . . ."

I turn the information over inside my brain, trying to make sense of it. Maybe I'm still a little fuzzy because it's so early in the morning, but it's like Thespis is speaking another language.

And for some reason the language annoys me. Even though the language is obviously about theater, it's like Thespis is trying to prove he's smarter than me. And he won't even look me in the eye.

I'm used to being invisible during the rest of the lonely year, when I'm just Stella's geeky little sister, but not during the summer. Not here at the Blue Moon.

And so abruptly I turn and head for the kitchen, without a word to Thespis.

He can show himself the ropes for all I care.

Breakfast Duty is my first chore of the day. The Blue Moon gives Free Room (that's a place to stay) and Board (that's food) to the actors and apprentices and techies. I'm in charge of Breakfast, but then a cook comes for Lunch and Dinner.

Breakfast is supposed to be out on the counter by eight thirty, since rehearsal usually begins at nine thirty. But mornings (like this one) after an Opening Night are always different. The actors get to sleep in late after the party. There won't be auditions and rehearsals for the next show for a couple of days.

I'm still supposed to have breakfast ready, though, just in case there are some early risers.

And so I'm doing the usual first thing—starting the coffee going—when I hear the kitchen door creak open and shut. Footsteps. I know Thespis is standing there, behind me. I can feel him. I wonder if he's seeing me now or if he's just contemplating the floor or the ceiling.

"What d-d-do we do first?" he asks.

"We?" I throw it back over my shoulder.

"You're showing me the r-ropes, r-right?"

"'Alack for mercy,'" I mumble under my breath, but I feel myself relenting.

I hate to admit it, but I have a hard time *not* doing what's expected of me. Stella says it's why I can't help but answer geeky questions in school and why I make such a good Gofer at the Blue Moon. She says it's why I chose Dad for the summer, instead of Mom, even though it made me feel mixed-up inside to be given the choice in the first place.

"You're a martyr," she informed me after Mom left. "You just love being Dad's little theater slave."

"So what are you?" I asked, annoyed.

"A star," she answered. "Dad's already promised me Miranda."

And so I begin showing Thespis the ropes. We go through the refrigerator and the cabinets, and I show him where to find all the breakfast stuff. Boxes of every kind of cereal under the sun, yogurt, bread and jam, peanut butter and honey. Cartons of milk and juice— apple, orange, grapefruit, tomato. Together we set everything out on the counter.

"Is this exactly what you d-d-do every morning?" Thespis asks.

"Well, Stella is *supposed* to take turns with Breakfast Duty," I reply, turning away from the counter to fill the electric tea kettle with water from the sink. "But my beloved sister has hardly lifted a finger around here since she got the role of Miranda, so I'm basically left doing all the chores, including answering the phone and helping Barbara the cook with lunch and dinner and working on the set when there's a new show to put up and doing Props and being a Gofer." I count off the list of duties on my fingers. "I get a very small allowance for all this, so obviously it's slave labor."

I glance over at Thespis, and I can't believe it! He's busy rearranging everything we've just set out on the counter. He's actually organizing the juice cartons into one perfect line, setting the various boxes of tea and different jars of jam into rows.

Onstage, Dad says it's the simple things an actor chooses to do—like plumping pillows on a couch, or smoothing a tablecloth, or lining things up on a counter—that make his or her character real, believable, interesting. Tiny actions that aren't necessarily written in the script. Business, it's called. An actor's business.

I cross my arms over my chest, silently watching the performance, Thespis's business.

Without seeming to realize he has an audience, he starts in on the cereal boxes, lining them up precisely, like he's playing a game of giant dominoes.

His expression is so intense—cheeks slightly sucked in, eyes narrowed—it's almost like he's in a trance. When he gets to the last box of cereal, his face loses some of its intensity. It seems to open, the muscles along the jaw softening. A tiny half smile—at least I think it's a smile, it's a little hard to tell—flashes for a brief second. And then—*poof*—it disappears.

And that's when Thespis seems to realize he's being watched. He doesn't look up, but his hands come to a stop and his cheeks bloom the color of Mama Duvall's early spring roses. The faintest blush of pink.

I wait for him to look at me, shrug, explain himself.

"It's eight thirty exactly," Thespis announces instead, gazing at a giant watch on his right wrist. "What do we do now?"

I don't answer right away. I'm fighting the sudden, overwhelming urge to reach out and knock the first cereal box over, just to see what would happen.

VII.

HERE'S HOW I SEE IT:

As a famous Broadway actress, there are so many demands on my time:

Appointments with hairdressers and stylists.

Sessions with a personal trainer to keep my body fit. (Being in good shape is very important to a stage actor.)

Interviews with newspapers and magazines.

Lunch with other famous people.

Acting lessons to hone my craft.

Voice lessons to perfect my instrument (that's the voice).

Rehearsals for new plays.

HERE'S HOW IT IS:

Office Duty. That's what comes next in my daily Blue Moon routine.

I'm supposed to sit at a desk in the office and answer the phone when it rings, take down reservations, answer questions about the plays and the theater.

In between the ringing of the phone I explain it all

to Thespis. I show him the seating chart and the list of ticket prices.

I don't actually let him answer the phone, though. I can't help but wonder about the stutter. Will it be worse on the phone? Will he be able to speak at all?

And what about when he goes onstage?

How can he truly be *quite the young thespian* with a stutter? Wouldn't standing in front of a whole audience of strangers make him nervous? Wouldn't it make the stutter worse?

"D-d-did you know that the shortest play ever is *Breath* by Samuel B-Becket?"

"My brother was named after Becket," I reply.

"D-d-did you know that *B-breath* has no d-dialogue and no actors and lasts only thirty-five seconds?"

I don't answer. I've only known the kid for about an hour total, and I've already noticed that he hardly ever waits for a response to his "questions." Plus, he's not even looking at me (surprise?). He's studying the wall of photos—shots from past productions, scenes going back to the very first season of the Blue Moon. Black and white because black and white is more dramatic, professional. Framed eight by tens. So many different faces. So many different actors. Sometimes an actor might return for a second season or a third, but a lot of times, it's a whole new company each new year.

Of course, my face is on the wall too. I wonder if Thespis will notice. I keep waiting for him to ask me about my life in the theater—because it's all there for anyone to see.

There are photos of me as a baby crawling in the background on the rehearsal room floor during various rehearsals. There's one of me at age two holding a skull next to my face, grinning from ear to ear just like the toothless head. (The skull was a Prop from *Hamlet*: "Alas, poor Yorick, I knew him . . .") There's a photo of my debut at age four as GIRL in a play my dad wrote himself (he's a playwright as well as an actor and director), and there's one of me a year later dressed as a little woodland sprite from *A Midsummer Night's Dream*.

My favorite photo is from *Medea* (one of the greatest tragedies of all time). It shows me at age eight lying on the stage floor, covered in blood (fake, of course), after my own mother (MEDEA) has killed me to take revenge on her unfaithful husband. (Actually MEDEA is supposed to kill two sons, but Dad merged the roles into one as he often does with kid parts and I cut my hair short to look like a boy. All great actors must be versatile!)

Mom hated the play because it was about a mother who kills her own kids and a bunch of other people too, but I loved it, even though it did give me the shivers sometimes. Every night I had to scream backstage while MEDEA (an actress named Linda) acted like she was stabbing me with a knife, and then I had to be splattered with this mixture of Karo syrup and food coloring and then carried bloody and lifeless out onto the stage.

The thing is, playing dead is not as easy as you'd think. I had to lie onstage for the whole last scene of the play—about fifteen minutes, which is really long when you're not supposed to move or even breathe. During the whole three-week run I was always worried that I would have to sneeze or cough, and sometimes I could feel something crawling up my leg, and I was terrified it was a wolf spider (really big, hairy spiders that seem to love the stage in summer).

I could tell all of this to Thespis, if he would ask, but he doesn't.

"The Blue Moon d–d–does a lot of tragedy," Thespis comments instead.

"Dad likes tragedy best," I reply, quickly adding, "And so do I."

Thespis turns slightly toward me, his eyes on the desk in front of me. "Why?" he asks.

"Well . . . because tragedy is sad and makes you cry."

Thespis cocks his head, like he's listening for something more.

"Because . . . because tragedy makes you think."

He's still waiting, and I feel myself panicking, which is completely stupid. I usually don't have any trouble telling people about my love for tragedy. And why do I care what Thespis thinks, anyway?

"The tragic roles are the best, the meatiest roles, for an actor to really sink her teeth into," I finally add. It's something Dad has always told me. "When I'm older I want to play all the great tragic roles—Juliet, Ophelia, Desdemona, Medea. . . ." My voice trails off, trying to think of more. I know that if Mom were here, she'd shake her head and click her tongue. She doesn't get my "obsession" with tragedy at all. She's always claimed I was an uncommonly happy baby, laughing inside her belly before I was born. And she's always trying to persuade Dad to do more comedies at the Blue Moon, plays that simply entertain, make people feel good.

But Dad says that he created the Blue Moon in order to do Real Theater, and that Real Theater shouldn't just make people feel good. Real theater should make people think.

"A great tragedy is one that gets to the very essence of man's existence," he'll say in his Explaining Voice (the one I love because it gives me chills). "A great tragedy makes you question life, question your place in the larger scheme of things."

I open my mouth to say all this to Thespis, but I don't get the chance.

"D-d-did you know that tragedy c-c-comes from the Greek word for 'goat song'?" Thespis asks.

"What does a 'goat song' have to do with tragedy?" I scoff.

Thespis shrugs. "I don't know."

The phone rings. I take down one reservation and then another. Thespis goes back to studying the photos.

We don't really speak again until Office Duty is over and Lunch Duty has begun.

"D-d-did you know that the audience often threw rotten vegetables at the actors in Shakespeare's d-day—if they d-didn't like the play?" Thespis asks while we're helping Barbara the cook cut up cucumbers for a salad.

"Do you see any rotten vegetables here?" Barbara asks sharply, giving Thespis a look of indignation. Barbara has been the cook here forever. She takes a lot of pride in the food she serves the actors. "We do not cook with rotten vegetables here at the Blue Moon. Those cucumbers came fresh out of my garden this morning!"

Thespis quickly shakes his head. His cheeks are blooming pink again.

"You don't have to worry about that anyway," I inform him. "I've seen people fall asleep or get up and leave during a performance at the Blue Moon because they didn't understand the play, but I've never seen any flying vegetables."

When lunch is served Thespis meets the whole cast and crew. We all sit together at tables lined up on the patio.

"How now?"

"What fun we had last night!"

"I'm worn out from dancing!"

Everyone is abuzz over Opening Night and the Opening Night party. At first they ignore Thespis as they talk and laugh about the things that happened onstage and after the play was over.

I love lunchtime and dinnertime. The whole cast and crew of the Blue Moon is like one big, loud, happy family.

At first Thespis is completely silent, staring down at his plate, barely eating, but after a while the actors begin to show some interest in him. They ask him questions about his life.

He was born in Ohio.

He has moved around a lot.

They came here to be close to family.

"D-d-d-did you know that in Shakespeare's day, theaters were built outside the city limits?" Thespis asks out of the blue when there's actually a moment of silence. "It's b-because plays were forbidden by the church. Actors could b-b-be thrown in jail for acting in p-plays."

Silence. I hold my breath, waiting to see what the whole group will make of such an announcement.

"Hey, that's pretty cool," Ray says. "So actors have always been kind of like renegades. Outlaws." He stands up and does an imitation of a gunslinger, and everybody laughs. "Cool info, dude." Ray reaches out and gives Thespis a soft punch on the arm. "What else do you know?"

Thespis starts rattling off more information, just like that. A walking, talking encyclopedia of theater history. All the actors ooh and aahh over each new tidbit.

And the more Thespis talks, the quieter I become. I sit at the table, silently picking at my food. The word "tragedy" pops into my head, and then "goat song." All at once I remember a story Mama Duvall told me, about Flossie, a baby goat she bottle-fed from birth because the mother had died. Flossie would follow Mama Duvall everywhere she went. If Mama Duvall went away from the farm, that little goat would just stand at the fence, bleating its little heart out.

"And that bleating sounded for all the world like a human child," Mama Duvall said, "like a baby crying for its mother."

One day while Mama Duvall was out running errands, a new neighbor thought it *was* a baby crying, and came over to see what he could do, but then he realized it was only a little old goat. Later he told her that the sound of that goat crying was so sorrowful, it just about broke his heart.

Maybe that's the reason the word "tragedy" comes from "goat song." Because both can break your heart.

VIII.

HERE'S HOW I SEE IT:

Thespis's mom comes to retrieve her son right after lunch.

"I missed my darling boy so very much," she cries, trapping him in an inescapable bear hug. "I don't think I can part with him ever, ever again. I'm sorry, but he won't be a Blue Moon intern after all."

HERE'S HOW IT IS:

It's my own dad who comes to retrieve Thespis after lunch.

I'm about to take Thespis on a tour of backstage, when Dad makes a sudden surprise appearance.

"Ah, there you are, young man," Dad's voice booms out. "Having fun so far? Junebug showing you the ropes?"

Thespis nods.

"Good, good!" Dad glances at his watch. "I have a bit of time now, so why don't you come this way? We can have a little chat. You can catch up with Junebug later." Dad reaches out and actually pats my head like I'm a good doggie.

"Woof, woof," I mumble, but Dad doesn't even notice.

He puts an arm around Thespis, and together they head for the office.

I stand totally still, watching them disappear around the corner. The tightness in my chest is back. A strange feeling, different from the knot. Like something pressing against my heart.

Abruptly I turn and head backstage, plucking up the beastie from the Prop Table as I pass by and making a beeline for my favorite place in the whole world: the Costume Room.

The Costume Room is where I know I will find my Favorite Person in the Whole Entire World.

SIMON LILY, *a genius when it comes to costume design; flamboyant (that means having a very showy appearance or manner); lives in New York City but has traveled all over the world.*

"June, *dahling!*" Simon exclaims when he sees me, throwing his arms into the air in greeting and planting two kisses—one for each cheek. (Very big city, very cosmopolitan.)

This is how Simon always greets me—as if he hasn't seen me in years (even though he just saw me at lunch). And he always calls me *dahling.* (Of course, he calls everyone *dahling,* but I happen to know I am his favorite *dahling* of all.)

Simon has been coming to the Blue Moon since before I was born. He was a friend of Dad's in New York, and he was here the first season to help Mom learn how to design costumes. Even though Mom can design her own costumes now, Simon still comes for at least part of the season. It appears he's staying the whole summer this year, although no one has actually said so out loud.

"What have we here?" Simon asks.

I hold out the beastie head. Simon clucks over the poor thing like a mother hen. He turns to ponder, finger to lips, the multitude of shelves and drawers that make up one entire wall of the Costume Room.

"Hmmm, let's see, where did I put that extra fur?" he murmurs, opening and closing drawers, rummaging through leftover swatches of fabric, zippers, buttons, and lace until he finds what looks like a squirrel's hide. "*Voilà!*" he cries.

Together we sit at the sewing table. The beastie goes on a wig stand. Simon gives little "mm-hmm's" of encouragement as I press on the snout to get the wrinkles out and glue more fur onto the bald patches.

"Did you have fun at the party last night, *dahling*?" Simon asks. "I don't think you stayed very long. I turned around and—*poof!*—you were gone."

The tightness returns. I've always loved Opening Night Parties. I've always tried to stay awake as long as I possibly can. But last night was different.

Dad wasn't himself at all. He wore that forgotten-line look all night. And when he asked Lelia to dance, the knot in my stomach pulled so tight I thought I was going to lose my cookies and punch, and so I had to exit the scene immediately.

"We missed Evvie, hmmm?" Simon asks softly.

I nod and concentrate hard on the beastie. My throat closes and my eyes fill with water. I feel like such a baby, even though it's Simon, someone I've known my entire life.

Shouldn't I be able to cry in front of Simon?

Shouldn't I be able to tell him what I'm thinking? That I do miss Evvie (my mom), and I don't understand why she wasn't here for Opening Night like always.

Shouldn't I be able to ask Simon what's going on with my family? Why Mom left, and why I had to choose between Mom and Dad for the summer?

Shouldn't I be able to ask Simon what happens when the summer ends?

I think Simon knows the questions are there. I can feel him waiting for me to ask them.

But for some reason I just can't. I keep my hands busy with the glue and fake fur. I swallow hard and blink back the tears.

Simon lets out a little sigh. "How about a spot of

tea, *dahling*? Just what we need, hmmm?" He rests a hand gently on my shoulder for a moment before heading to the back room to start the electric tea kettle and arrange the ornate silver cups and saucers and teapot on a silver tray.

The grand tea set is a Prop from shows past, and the tea party is something Simon and I have done since I was a very little girl. We sip from the ornate silver cups and Simon tells me about the places he's lived: New York City, Paris, Istanbul, and Marrakech. He tells me about the stars he's designed costumes for, which ones are *just dahling* and which ones are *simply horrid*. He tells me about the sights he's seen and the people he's met on his exotic travels: kings and queens, dukes and duchesses—real ones, not just characters out of something by Shakespeare.

He also tells me things about myself, things that make me warm inside, just like the tea.

"When Evvie brought you back from the hospital the day after you were born," Simon begins now, my favorite story about myself, one I've heard a hundred times but never get tired of hearing, "she put you in a basket at her feet so she could keep sewing, because she wasn't finished with the costumes for the play about the Scotsman, and as you know . . ."

This is my cue to chant, "The show must go on!" just like Dad always says.

"You were such a good baby, an angel, *dahling*! But if you did start to fuss, she'd simply slide you under a row of costumes from seasons past so you could gaze up at all the colors hanging overhead. And you would stop your crying, immediately. And you'd be content for hours. We'd check on you constantly, of course, and there you were, just staring up with those big dark eyes at the lovely costumes above you."

"Which costumes did I like the best?" I ask, even though I know.

"Ah, *Romeo and Juliet*!" he replies.

See? I loved tragedy from the very beginning!

"We'd done the play the season before. Just gorgeous, if I do say so myself. All that golden brocade! All those teensy weensy mirrors Evvie and I sewed into the fabric *by hand*!" Simon pauses for emphasis. *"By hand."* He shakes his head, gazing off into the past. "Some of our very best work."

We are silent now, sipping our tea. Simon always

makes mine with lots of milk and honey.

"In the olden days people used to believe that you could tell a person's future by reading the tea leaves left over in the bottom of their cup." Simon is gazing down into his cup, and so I gaze down into mine. There are a few soggy dark spots on the bottom. I stare at them, moving the cup one way and then the other.

Maybe the tea leaves will tell me what will happen at the end of the summer, if Mom will come home, if everything will go back to the way it used to be.

Maybe the tea leaves will tell me something about Thespis. Like why he had to appear—*poof!*—out of nowhere.

"How are you getting along with our new intern?"

Maybe the tea leaves told Simon what I was thinking!

"'A strange fish.'"

The line pops out. It's from *The Tempest*. Something one of the characters calls CALIBAN because he is such an odd creature, only half human.

"Now, *dahling*, it's not easy coming into a new place, making new friends."

"He didn't seem to have any trouble at lunch," I mumble, remembering how the actors seemed to hang on his every word.

Simon raises one eyebrow high above the other. It's one of my favorite expressions. I always try to imitate it, but I can never get the one eyebrow to obey without the other going up too.

"Let's give the boy a chance, shall we?" Simon says in a quiet but firm voice.

"'Let's throw the man overboard,'" I reply (*The Tempest* again).

The one eyebrow goes impossibly high. I let out a resigned sigh and give a nod. It's especially hard not to do what Simon Says.

"Good girl." Simon starts to rise, but stops and takes my hands between his. "'A strange fish . . . ,'" he says thoughtfully. "You know, *dahling*, we're all 'strange fish' here. That's the wonderful thing about the theater. We may feel like outsiders in the real world. We may feel like fish out of water." Simon pauses and gives me a meaningful look, which makes the tears threaten again. Simon knows all about how out of water I feel during the rest of the year. "But in the world of the theater, we all find a home. Everyone is welcome here."

Simon squeezes my hands and then leans in to plant a kiss on my forehead. As he stands to clear the tea set away, I turn his words over inside my brain.

It's hard to imagine Simon feeling like an outsider. He's so confident, so sure of himself. He's traveled all over the world. He's dined with royalty. But then I remind myself how some people turn and stare at him here, in this small town, when we're out running errands.

I look at Simon and try to see him as a total stranger might—but I can't really do it. His perfectly shaved head, his pierced ears with the tiny silver loops in both lobes, the way he wears Japanese kimonos or colorful caftans over crisp jeans or shiny cotton trousers, the elegant leather sandals that most men around here wouldn't be caught dead in. I know these things are what make Simon *a strange fish* here in the middle of nowhere, but to me they are what make him Simon.

"Anon, *dahling*," Simon calls over his shoulder, balancing the tea tray in one hand like a waiter in some fancy restaurant.

"Anon," I call back, but I'm not sure where I should anon *to*.

Part of me wants to walk the three miles, across the fields, to Mama Duvall's house to see Mom. I haven't seen her in days—since before *The Tempest* opened— and that was only for a quick lunch because we were so busy getting ready for Opening Night. If I go to the farm for the rest of the day, I'd definitely avoid Thespis and the whole "showing him the ropes" thing. But I'd also avoid all my other Blue Moon duties, and I just can't imagine actually doing that. Maybe I am a martyr, a theater slave, just like Stella said, but I can't let Dad down.

I reach for the beastie, careful not to touch the places where the glue is still drying, and slip it over my head. I stalk through backstage, growling, a terrible, ferocious beast. When I get to the middle of the forest (center stage), I lean my head back and howl at the sky, just like CALIBAN does during the play.

"D-did you know that some of the earliest Greek theaters were built almost exactly like this one?"

Thespis steps out from behind a tree.

I turn and let out a roar.

Let's give the boy a chance, shall we?

But it's just a little roar.

IX.

HERE'S HOW I SEE IT:

The Blue Moon was built in the middle of a great big city where everybody loves theater and they all come out in droves to see each new play.

HERE'S HOW IT IS:

The Blue Moon was built in the middle of a great big field.

Mama Duvall gave the field to Mom and Dad as a wedding present, even though Dad still thought he'd be taking his new bride back to New York City. After Beck was born though, Dad did try to do a little farming—a big garden, a few cows and goats. But farming didn't really suit him.

So one day, after Stella was born, he decided that instead of growing corn and tobacco and soybeans (the things people usually grow around here) he'd grow a theater.

Of course everybody around here thought Dad was nuts, but they were kind of used to his crazy notions. After all, he was the first ever Cantrell to refuse to go to law school (in a small town everybody knows everything about you and your entire family). He was the only Cantrell—the only local kid—who had ever been on Broadway (once!).

So when Dad first started putting his plan into motion, folks would just come and stand around and stare as Dad began digging a big hole in the middle of the field with a borrowed bulldozer.

"What's the big hole for?" they'd ask.

And Dad would tell them about the Greeks and how the first Greek amphitheaters were built into hollowed-out hillsides.

"Aren't you going to have a roof?" they'd ask.

And Dad would explain about the Greeks again and how they performed in nature, outside under the sun, moon, and stars.

"Who's going to act in these plays?" they'd ask.

And Dad would explain about his plan to bring actors from New York City for a whole summer and have them perform a bunch of different plays.

"Where are all these actors going to stay?" they'd ask.

And Dad would explain that he wanted to build a

kind of dormitory right next to the stage so that the actors wouldn't have to go anywhere. They would be able to live and breathe theater all summer long.

Most of the townies (as we call them) didn't really understand why anybody would want to live and breathe theater all summer long, but they started to help Dad anyway. I guess they got tired of standing around watching him work so hard. One day they just started working too, and then they started bringing Dad things that would help to build the Blue Moon.

Like one time somebody had a dump truck full of bricks from an old house that had been torn down, and so they brought it to my dad so he could build the amphitheater into the hillside like he talked about.

And somebody else brought some old lumber that had come from another building being torn down. And Dad used that to build the dorm rooms.

And one day a guy showed up with half a cement truck full of cement because he said somebody had ordered too much and he'd just have to get rid of it anyway. So that's how the Blue Moon ended up with a concrete stage.

And one day somebody else showed up with a

bunch of old windows that were being replaced with new windows, and Dad put the old windows into the rooms he was building with the old lumber.

After a full year of everybody helping out, the theater was finished more or less, and Dad got some actor friends of his to come down for the summer to put on some plays.

"This is everybody's theater!" Dad proclaimed on the very first Opening Night.

And at first it was.

X.

HERE'S HOW I SEE IT:

Like all serious actors, each night before I make my grand entrance onstage, I go through my preshow ritual.

1. I drink a cup of steaming water with one spoonful of honey and one slice of lemon in it. (This soothes the voice.)
2. I do some stretching exercises to limber up my body. (Being relaxed is very important onstage.)

3. I do a series of voice exercises to warm up my voice. (The voice is the actor's most important instrument, as Dad always says.)

4. I put on my face (that's the makeup part).

5. I shake out my costume (wolf spiders love to hide in costumes) before slipping it on.

6. I gather 'round with my fellow cast members, and we hold hands and have a moment of silence before the Stage Manager calls "Places." (The moment of silence is not a prayer really, at least not the kind you say on Sunday. It's a nod to the Theater Gods, as Dad always says. A wish. The kind you make on birthdays before you blow out the candles on your cake. A wish for good things to happen and for everyone to remember their lines.)

HERE'S HOW IT IS:

I swing my arms back and forth and roll my wrists in circles in preparation for my (behind-the-scenes) being Thunder. All around me the actors are going through the last-minute bits of their own preshow rituals. I close my eyes and listen to all the different voices warming up.

"Me-me-me-me-me-me-me."

"La-la-la-la-la-la-la." (Going up the scale and back down again.) "La-la-la-la-la-la-la-la."

"Moo-moo-moo-moo-moo-moo-moo."

"How now, brown cow?"

I don't hear Dad's voice in the crazy chorus, but I know he's out back behind the Dressing Rooms warming up with one of his favorite Shakespeare speeches:

> All the world's a stage,
> And all the men and women merely players;
> They have their exits and their entrances;
> And one man in his time plays many parts . . .

It's one of his favorite monologues, whether we're doing Shakespeare or not. It's part of his pre-show ritual, his good-luck charm.

"Places!"

Enter Coleman, her voice tolling like a bell over all the other sounds.

COLEMAN, *one name only; a light in the dark, Dad calls her, because she was named for a lamp, but also because she's like a lighthouse on a stormy sea; as Stage Manager, she is the one who keeps everything running smoothly during the show.*

"Places," she calls again, and all the actors scurry to their places to wait to make their entrance.

"Break a leg! Break a leg!"

The voices ring out.

"Break a wrist," CALIBAN/Ray growls at me as he passes by.

"Ha, ha, very funny," I reply, taking my place next to my sheet of tin.

"D-do you know why actors say, 'Break a leg'?" Thespis asks. He's been shadowing me the whole time, but he's been strangely quiet in all the hubbub, a peculiar look on his face, almost like he's frightened.

"So they won't actually break a leg onstage," I reply.

"Ballet d-dancers say *merde*, which is French for . . ." His voice trails off and his cheeks bloom pink.

"I know what *merde* means," I inform him, without bothering to add that I think it's weird that ballet dancers don't just say "Break a leg" too, since breaking a leg for a ballet dancer would be pretty catastrophic.

"Fade lights," Coleman murmurs, and then she turns and gives me the signal. "Cue Thunder."

I do my usual crash and bang. When the storm is over, I take a bow. Even though Thespis isn't really looking at me, as usual. He's looking at the sheet of tin.

"D-did you know that the Victorians were the first to use the Thunder sheet b-behind the scenes to create the s-sound of thunder?"

"Um, no."

"They also created the g-g-glass crash. It's a b-box full of broken g-glass—"

"I know what a glass crash is," I interrupt. "I made one when I was, like, nine years old." My voice sounds harsh, even to my own ears.

Let's give the boy a chance, shall we?

"I'll show it to you if you want," I add.

Thespis nods, and we head to the Prop Room, where all the Props are kept from shows past. Hundreds of Props, jumbled together on the floor and on shelves lining the walls. The Prop Room is jam-packed with furniture, too, old couches andchairs, tables and desks, a couple of out-of-tune pianos. Used furniture we've collected over the years, from yard sales or whenever people are just getting rid of stuff.

Thespis doesn't seem to know where to look first. He stops near a piano and makes a slow, full circle, his eyes wide.

I rummage through a couple of shelves, finally finding the crash box, covered in dust. I sneeze a couple of times as I carefully slide it out and carry it over to Thespis. It's a cardboard box with layers of tape around it to keep the broken glass inside from ripping into the cardboard.

"We broke old bottles and glasses into a trash can and then put all the pieces into this box and taped it up," I explain, giving it just the tiniest of shakes so that Thespis can at least get a sense of what's inside without making enough noise to be heard onstage.

"D-d-did you know the Victorians used a b-bucket?"

I just stare at him.

"For the glass crash."

"I guess they didn't have cardboard boxes back then, huh?"

Thespis shakes his head.

"How do you remember all that stuff, anyway?" I ask.

"My dad used to say I had a photographic memory."

"What does that mean? Photographic memory?"

"It means I c-c-can read something once and then remember it."

"That must come in handy when you're memorizing lines, right?"

Thespis doesn't answer right away. His gaze shifts from the crash box to his feet.

"R-r-right."

"Junebug, are you in there?"

It's Stella, her voice a mere whisper from the doorway, but I know a gofer search when I hear one. Carefully I return the crash box to its place on the shelf.

"I need a safety pin, like, now," Stella whispers frantically. "The button came off of my skirt, and I can't find Simon anywhere."

"Okay, okay."

"I'll be in the Dressing Room."

"Yes, milady."

Thespis shadows me as I obey Stella's command, and he shadows me as I gofer more requests: water, ice, Props, cigarettes, matches.

"Is this exactly what you d-d-do every night?" he asks during a lull in the gofering.

"Pretty much, yeah."

"D-d-does everybody ask for pretty much the same thing every night, then?"

"Well, no. . . ." I give a quick sideways glance to see if he's serious. It's kind of a strange question. Why would the actors ask for the same thing every night? "You never know what you'll be gofering for next." I shrug. "You just have to be ready for anything."

"B-b-b-but how d-do you know where to find everything?"

Now Thespis is looking really worried.

"Well, I grew up here, so of course I know where everything is," I reply, and then I bite my lip.

Let's give the boy a chance, shall we?

"But it's not that hard to figure out where stuff is," I quickly add. "And you can always ask somebody. Like me."

Thespis doesn't look relieved, exactly.

"Come on, let's watch the rest of the play," I suggest, and Thespis follows me to the wings.

Onstage, the characters are getting ready to leave the island and go back to Milan. MIRANDA/Stella is thrilled that she finally gets to see the real world, but you can tell PROSPERO/Dad is a little mixed about it. You can tell he really doesn't want to leave all the magic behind.

I know exactly how he feels.

XI.

HERE'S HOW I SEE IT:

The curtain falls for the night on my huge Broadway hit. Flowers rain down on my head. Friends gather in my dressing room after the show to congratulate me. Fans wait for me outside the stage door.

"Ms. Cantrell, you were magnificent tonight!"

"Ms. Cantrell, you are an inspiration!"

I try to sign as many autographs as possible before my agent hurries me to my waiting car.

"Ms. Cantrell must rest now," she says to the crowd. "You must understand. The play is so very demanding."

My driver takes me home to my hip downtown

loft. There are flowers everywhere, from my countless admirers. There are close friends everywhere—actors, directors, artists—and we sit up all night long, talking about life and art and theater.

HERE'S HOW IT IS:

The house is dark and empty. And so I go through every room.

"Lights up!" I command in a Coleman voice, flipping switches, illuminating every dark space.

I hate the dark.

In the kitchen I search the fridge and cabinets, hungry as any MARINER alone on a storm-tossed sea, but (*alas, alack*) the shelves are bare, except for some old milk and moldy cheese and an inch of peanut butter.

All summer long we eat at the Blue Moon (Free Room and Board!), but Mom always made sure there were snacks at home. I ate very little before the show tonight. I heard one of the actresses explaining to Thespis why she never eats supper. She said that actors should be pure and empty when they perform. So I tried it (even though I don't exactly go onstage). Now

I am starved, and the inch of peanut butter doesn't help much.

Alack for mercy!

With a woefully empty belly I trudge down the hallway toward my room, pausing for a moment at my parents' door.

A scene from last year—from every year of my life before this one—plays itself out inside my head.

MEMORY SCENE I

[MOM and JUNEBUG snuggle together among the fluffy pillows of the huge cherry bed. They are the first home from the Blue Moon after the night's performance, and they are talking about how the play went that night, how the actors performed, which actors they like and which actors are harder to like. After a while, BECK and STELLA enter the scene, perching on the edge of the bed, joining in on the conversation. At last DAD makes his grand entrance after making sure the

Blue Moon is settled for the night,
quoting something from Shakespeare
as he slides into bed, gathering his
family up into one big puppy pile.
He has not showered yet, and so he
smells of sweat and makeup, and there
is makeup staining the neckline of his
old T-shirt, but all these things make
him more endearing. The FAMILY lies
together, laughing and talking, deep
into the night, until JUNEBUG drifts
off into blissful slumber.]

The scene fades. I feel an ache that goes deeper than
any pang of hunger.

I start to turn away from the empty bed, and that's
when the phone rings, scaring me nearly to death.

A crazy killer calling to tell me he knows I'm
alone?

A stupid prank?

Thespis calling to impart one more piece of information before he goes to sleep?

"Junebug?"

It's Mom, her voice all sleepy. And the sound—so familiar, so . . . yummy—makes the ache even deeper. I lie down on the bed, holding the phone close.

"Hey, how's my sweetie? I hoped I'd catch you before you went to bed."

"Okay," I manage, even the usual knot has somehow moved to my throat.

"How's the show going?"

"Okay."

"How's Stella?"

"Okay." I take a deep breath. "She was nervous at first, but she's warmed up now." Another breath. "You should have come for Opening."

There's a long pause. A pregnant pause, Dad would call it if he were directing this scene.

"And how is my Thunder?" Mom asks, her voice suddenly too cheerful.

"Thunderous."

Mom laughs, her deep laugh—a wondrous sound.

"Is Cass there with you?"

I don't answer right away, and then, "He's in the shower." The words come out in a rush.

There's another long, pregnant pause. Mom has always said she can tell when I'm not being completely truthful. My cheeks give me away. I'm a blusher just like Thespis, only I usually go all the way to tomato red. I know I'm blushing now, but of course Mom can't see that. I wonder if she can tell over the phone anyway. I don't know why I lied.

"Are you going to come over Sunday?" Mom's voice is too cheerful again, too eager. "Mama Duvall said she'd make banana pudding."

Banana pudding—made the old-fashioned way with real bananas and fluffy meringue—is my all-time favorite. But something makes me hold back. I don't know what it is.

"Well, I might be busy, you know. . . ."

Another lie. The first Sunday after a play has opened is a Free Sunday. No rehearsals. No Breakfast, Lunch, or Dinner Duty. No show that night.

"Okay, Junebug." Mom's voice is quieter now. "Whatever you want to do. It's okay with me. It really is. But I'd like to see you. I miss you."

Tears threaten like a storm. I shut my eyes and push them back. Even though no one's here to see.

"A serious actor must be strong!" Dad always says. "A serious actor must be in control of his or her emotions at all times."

"I love you, Junebug," Mom whispers.

I want to tell Mom I love her back. I want to tell her that I miss her and that I don't understand why she isn't here. But all I can manage to say is, "Okay. Good night."

After I've hung up, I stay curled on Mom's side of the bed for a long time. I realize that the pillow still smells like her—the shampoo and face cream she uses.

When I finally get up and go down the hall to my own room, I carry the pillow with me. I head straight for bed. I lie in the semidark, my face against my mom's pillow, staring at my Manhattan night-light glowing in one corner.

I know it's babyish to still use a night-light, but I like falling asleep gazing at the grand skyline. I bought the night-light years ago, on a trip to the city.

Every spring we all go to New York with Dad so he can audition actors for the Blue Moon season. (Believe it or not, New York actors actually want to leave the city for the summer and act in the middle of nowhere.) This year was different, though. Dad made the trip alone. Mom said it was because money was tight, but there was something else, too. It was like Dad wanted to be by himself.

I focus on the Manhattan glow and will myself to stay awake till Dad and Stella come home from "winding down" with the actors after the show. But I don't make it.

XII.

HERE'S HOW I SEE IT:

Stella wakes up extra early the next morning and sets out breakfast.

"I know I've been unfair, Junebug. Can you ever forgive me?" she pleads. "I promise I will set out breakfast for the rest of the season."

"O my kind sister, that's not necessary," I tell her. "We can still take turns."

"O no, I wouldn't dream of having you do more work!" Stella cries.

HERE'S HOW IT IS:

Stella is sleeping late. Again. I can hear her high, squeaky snore through the closed door.

Hard to believe that Beauty actually snores. O how she would hate for the news to get out!

I stand at the door a moment longer, but I don't even bother to knock, to try to wake her up. To tell her that it's been her turn for days now to do Breakfast Duty. I know it would be useless.

And so I head to Blue Moon for the usual routine. When I enter the kitchen, I'm stunned to find that Breakfast has already been served!

Wow, did the scene inside my head actually come true? Did Stella wake up extra early and then go home again just to fool me?

But then I notice the boxes of cereal. They're all in a perfect row.

"D-d-did you know that some people believe that Shakespeare didn't write all those plays?" Thespis asks, coming out of the pantry with a last carton of milk.

Now I'm the one gazing down at the floor. I know I should feel grateful. I've complained (to myself) for weeks about doing all the chores around here. I know

I should feel relieved that somebody else wants to help out for a change.

But I don't.

"Some p-p-people think that somebody else wrote the plays, not the man known as William Shakespeare."

"What are you talking about?"

Now I do look up. Thespis is focused on that last carton of milk—making sure it's perfect in its row.

"Everybody knows Shakespeare wrote those plays." I can hear how annoyed I sound, but I can't control it. "I mean, it says, 'by William Shakespeare,' right there on the script."

"No, you're quite right, young man."

Enter Dad. He's dressed in his usual summer attire when not onstage: Blue Moon Playhouse T-shirt and faded jeans, flip-flops. His dark hair is still wet from a shower, combed back away from his face. He hasn't shaved this morning, so there's some dark stubble along his cheeks and chin.

"Some people believe that a boy from a small town in England, son of a merchant, couldn't possibly have gone on to write such beautiful, timeless works." Dad is speaking in his Explaining Voice. He heads to the coffeepot and pours himself a cup.

"So who wrote the plays, then?" I ask.

Dad nods toward Thespis. "Who do you think wrote the plays, young man?"

"Well, m-maybe it was Marlowe."

"Ah yes, that's what some believe."

"Who's Marlowe?" I ask.

"Another playwright of the same time period. A friend and rival of Shakespeare's. But Marlowe died in a tavern brawl before many of Shakespeare's finest plays were written." Dad blows steam from his coffee and takes a tentative sip. "Some believe it might have been a nobleman in the queen's court. Someone who didn't want his own name used on the plays because it would have been unseemly for a person in his position to write plays."

"Why?" I ask.

"Because plays were considered vulgar—for commoners, not for the rich." Dad pauses. "Some even believe that Queen Elizabeth herself was the true Shakespeare!"

"But why don't people know for sure?" I ask. "I mean,

isn't there proof? Aren't there scripts or manuscripts or whatever with Shakespeare's name on them?"

"Well, it's a bit complicated, Junebug." Dad's voice has changed; it's still the Explaining Voice, but it's like he's explaining something to a two-year-old. "This is all ancient history in terms of actual documentation. Plays weren't printed in books, like they are today."

"B-B-Ben Jonson was the first to print the plays of Shakespeare," Thespis says.

"Ah, yes, that's right!" Dad beams across the counter at Thespis. "Another contemporary of Shakespeare's and another name bandied about as the true author."

"B-b-b-but they say that Jonson identified the author of the p-p-plays he printed as 'Sweet Swan of Avon.'"

"Right again!"

The words fly back and forth across the counter. Different theories, different names and plays. I feel like I'm at a tennis match, watching the ball. Thespis says something and Dad exclaims over it, adding to it, sending it back over the net.

After a while I lose track of the game. The words

start to blend together. The scene continues, but I'm not part of the conversation anymore. I'm not even there.

XIII.

HERE'S HOW I SEE IT:

Newspaper headlines across the world shout out: FAMOUS ACTRESS DISCOVERS TRUE IDENTITY OF SHAKESPEARE!

TV crews and reporters flock to my door.

"How did you discover the truth?" they shout out. "No one else has been able to solve this mystery for hundreds of years!"

"Well, it really wasn't that hard," I reply modestly. "The answer was always there. You just had to know where to look."

HERE'S HOW IT IS:

I exit the scene without a good-bye. Dad and Thespis don't even notice anyway.

I head straight to the Blue Moon library. It's a small room near the office—one of the only air-conditioned places—where we keep copies of plays we've done before, along with some history books and books about set design and lighting and sound.

I find the big book of Shakespeare—all the plays in one leather-bound collection—and ease it from the shelf. A bit dusty, so I wipe it down with the bottom of my T-shirt. I take a seat on the couch and open the book, paging through the beginning. There's an introduction, but skimming it, I don't see anything about William Shakespeare not actually being the author of the plays.

I keep flipping through the pages. So many plays! I've sometimes thought I might like to be a playwright, too, not just an actor. My dad writes plays along with everything else he does—act, direct, run a theater. (*Plenty of time to rest in the grave!*) So I guess it's in my blood. But I can't really imagine writing so many plays!

Did the man known as William Shakespeare really write so many? How did he come up with so many different characters, so many different plots?

In school last year we had to do a lot of writing, and my English teacher's favorite phrase was, "Write what you know!" But how could one person know so much? Shakespeare's plays are about kings and queens, magical creatures and deserted islands and foreign cities and war. And love. I know a lot of the plays are about love. Doomed love. Like *Romeo and Juliet*.

I close my eyes and see myself as JULIET on a stage, kneeling over the dead body of my beloved, ROMEO, poised to thrust the dagger deep into my heart.

"Hey Junebug, how's it going?"

I open my eyes and it's like a real-life ROMEO has appeared—*poof!*—just like that.

SCOTT STEVENS, *our young leading man; blond hair, blue eyes; absolutely gorgeous; and a great actor to boot.*

I can only stare. No words at all. It's like my brain has stopped working. It's like my mouth has stopped working too.

This is what always happens when Scott actually talks to me. I become completely stupid.

And my face turns the exact shade of tomato.

Scott plays FERDINAND in *The Tempest*. "'A thing divine,'" Stella calls him—onstage and off.

"What're you reading?" Scott asks in his laid-back way, coming closer, squinting at the book in my lap.

"Um, this," I manage to say (brilliant!), shutting the book so Scott can read the cover for himself.

"Brushing up on your Shakespeare?"

"Um, yeah."

"So, what's your favorite play?"

"Um . . ." My brain goes totally blank. "Um . . ." I try again, flipping the book open and saying the first title I see, without really thinking. "*Cymbeline*."

"Oh, yeah?" Scott perches on the arm of the couch (only a foot away from me!). "I've never read that one. What's it about?"

I don't know!

That's what I *should* say. Because I've never read it either. I didn't even know Shakespeare wrote a play called *Cymbeline* until this very moment.

What is wrong with me? Why couldn't I have just said *Romeo and Juliet*? The easiest to remember, the one I was thinking of when Scott arrived!

"Um . . ." I know my face is beyond tomato now. Maybe it's beet. "Well, it's about . . ."

Enter STELLA.

And what perfect timing! I know she's going to enjoy embarrassing me in front of the "thing divine."

"Oh, hey, Scott, I thought you might be here." She gives him her luscious smile. The one she's perfected by spending hours in front of the mirror. It turns most guys around here to mush. "I wondered if you, like, wanted to run some scenes for the audition tomorrow?"

"Oh, yeah, that would be great," Scott says, smiling but not (I'm happy to say) turning to mush. "Just a minute, though. Your little sis was just telling me about *Cymbeline*, her favorite Shakespeare play."

"Oh, really?" Stella's blue eyes pin me to the couch. "*Cymbeline*, huh?"

I hold my breath, waiting for her to tell Scott she doubts I've even read *Cymbeline*, but she only crosses her arms over her chest and smiles at me. A beautiful, evil smile.

"Go ahead, June*bug*, tell us what's the play about. I'm *dying* to hear."

I stare down at the book on my lap, blinking a few times, and then I flip to the start of the play where they always list the cast of characters.

"It's about, um, CYMBELINE, um . . . a king, and um, what happens when . . . um, it's about his daughter, too. . . . Her name is IMOGEN. . . ." I take a deep breath. "You know, it's kind of compli-cated, lots of mistaken identity and stuff." The words all mash together in a rush. I glance sideways at Scott. He's nodding his head, waiting for more. I slam the book closed. "Do you know that, um, some people don't think Shakespeare actually wrote the plays?"

Scott's eyes go wide with surprise. "Yeah. You know, I think I've heard that before!"

"You know, um, some people think that some-body else—maybe somebody more educated—um, wrote them, maybe . . ." My voice trails off. I hope he doesn't ask me who I think actually wrote the plays, because I can't remember the name of the playwright from Shakespeare's day that Dad and Thespis were talking about.

"Wow, what are you, like twelve or something?" Scott asks.

"I'm, um, almost thirteen," I manage to mumble, sitting a little taller in my seat.

"Dude, I didn't know anything about Shakespeare at thirteen," Scott says, shaking his head in wonder. "I was, like, into skateboarding and surfing and stuff. I wasn't into reading much at all. Nothing like this." He taps the book. "Pretty cool, Junebug."

"Um, thanks." I look down at the book in my lap again. I feel something gnawing at my insides—a tiny animal with tiny teeth. I know it must be guilt. Guilt over using Thespis's information, stuff I don't really know anything about. But when I glance up at Scott, he's giving me the most amazing smile. (He truly is a "thing divine.")

And so I ignore the gnawing and I ignore the fact that Stella is staring daggers at me from across the room (probably miffed that I've totally impressed Scott).

None of that matters right now. The only thing that matters is that I'm not invisible anymore.

XIV.

HERE'S HOW I SEE IT:

June Olivia Cantrell—written in golden letters on the door.

This is Broadway, and so of course I have my own personal Dressing Room. With my own personal makeup artist and dresser to help transform me into someone else.

HERE'S HOW IT IS:

Two Dressing Rooms. One for the Ladies and one for the Men.

Everybody shares at the Blue Moon. Even the bathrooms. (One for the Ladies and one for the Men.)

"How now, Junebug?"

Mimi is the only actress left in the Ladies' Dressing Room, putting on her face. (She plays CERES, an *airy spirit*, so she doesn't enter until Act II.)

MIMI RUSSELL, *our older leading lady; glamorous, gracious, a diva with a heart of gold; still beautiful despite her age, which is unknown since age is something "an actress never reveals."*

"I brought your drink, Mimi," I say, setting a teacup on the dressing table.

It's the third night of *The Tempest*, and the play is really starting to hum. I've already rolled thunder, and now I'm doing my gofering.

"Oh, you are such a dear, sweet girl!" Mimi cries, throwing two air kisses at me in the mirror. "So thoughtful! Thank you from the bottom of my heart." She takes a tentative sip of the steaming drink. "Perfect!" she proclaims. "Thank you, thank you!"

Mimi is the one who told me about the hot water with just a hint of lemon and a teaspoon of honey. She says all great actors use it to soothe their voices before they go onstage.

"You're welcome." I take a seat beside her. I know Thespis is waiting for me in the Green Room outside the Ladies' Dressing Room. I told him boys were forbidden inside, although that's not really true. Simon comes into the Ladies' Dressing Room all the time to fix costumes or just gossip with the Ladies. But I wanted to be shadowless for a while. I've hardly had a minute to myself.

I watch as Mimi rummages through the great black toolbox on the table in front of her. But of course it's no ordinary toolbox, no ordinary tools.

Three whole tiers of makeup—greasepaint, they used to call it in the old days of theater (I know this without Thespis telling me, thank you very much).

Tubes of foundation, sticks of rouge, cylinders of powder, a kaleidoscope of pencils for lining the eyes and the lips, brushes of all sizes, all kinds of lipstick. There are even fake eyelashes and eyebrows and coils of fake hair.

Tools of the actor's trade, as Dad likes to say.

In the world of theater every serious actor starts collecting his or her own box of tools, adding to it over the years. Dad gave me my own box for my eighth birthday, and slowly I'm doing the collecting. I keep my toolbox here in the Dressing Room even though I don't need a "face" for rolling thunder. I go and get it now and pop it open, just to look inside.

Not nearly as much makeup as Mimi, but then Mimi has been acting for more than twenty years.

"How's the audience tonight?" Mimi asks as she rouges her cheeks.

"Good," I quickly reply. Mimi is like Ray—she treats me like an adult, takes my opinions seriously. "They're pretty attentive, and they're getting the jokes."

"Excellent!" Mimi leans close to the mirror, working on her eyes. A bold slash of green, then blue and silver all the way up to the arched brows. Black kohl to line the lids.

When she's finished with her face, she turns for my approval.

"What do you think, my sweet, a little too much green?"

"No, I think it's perfect."

She reaches out and gives my cheek a soft caress. "You're just a dear!" she breathes airily, and then rises to find her costume on the rack behind us. She gives it a good shake.

"No wolf spiders!" she announces. "Did you know there was one in my costume last night before I put it on?" She shudders. "Awful things!"

"Awful," I repeat, mirroring her shudder.

Mimi slides the shimmery gown over the slip she's wearing. Simon created the costume from green silk and golden organza, and it makes Mimi look exactly as she should: like the queen of the fairies. She turns her back to me so I can help with the zipper. Then she gives a whirl in front of the mirror, letting the full skirt swirl around her.

"How do I look?" She strikes a pose.

"Like a queen," I answer.

"Ah, thank you, dear." She blows two more air kisses in my direction and exits the scene.

I sit back in my seat, wondering what to do next. I

can hear Thespis's voice. He must be saying something to Mimi, but I can't make out the words. I hear her laugh—a tinkling bell of a laugh. I roll my eyes à la Stella.

I feel like a turtle inside its shell, but I decide to stay in the Ladies' Dressing Room a while longer to avoid my shadow. I pull my toolbox closer, take up a new makeup sponge, and start to smooth on a layer of pale foundation evenly over my face.

"A blank slate!" Dad always says at this stage.

Next it's a bit of pink blush rubbed into the apples of my cheeks. I lean in close to the mirror—just like Mimi—to work on my eyes. A few slashes of green, like Mimi, but I can't quite get the eyeliner. It zigzags away from the lid.

I'm wiping it off with a Kleenex so I can start again when Lelia appears.

"Hey, Junebug!" Lelia takes her usual seat a few chairs down from me and opens a box of face powder, dusting her face and neck and arms lightly with a powder puff. "It's really hot out there tonight! My face is melting! I wish we had air conditioning."

"Theater under the stars!" I mumble, one of Dad's

favorite phrases when promoting the Blue Moon.

"I know, I know." Lelia gives a quick smile in the mirror. "And I have to admit it's pretty neat, performing outside in nature. I've never done it before. But I guess you're used to it, huh?"

I nod my head. As Lelia touches up her lipstick, I dart a glance at her in the mirror.

As ARIEL she wears a white leotard covered with silvery gauze and hundreds of white feathers and sequins like tiny stars. Her long black hair is pulled tightly back with feathers and sequins for a crown. She looks like a ballerina and a magnificent exotic bird both.

Lelia catches me watching her in the mirror and gives me another smile.

I feel my face heating up, and quickly I turn back to my own reflection to try the eyeliner again.

"Hey, want some help? Lining the eyes is really tough. It took me a long time to get the hang of it." She slides over to the seat next to me.

I don't really want her help, but I don't know how to say no without being completely rude.

"Okay." I hand her the liner, and she turns me to face her.

"Now close your eyes," she says.

I do as I'm told, and I feel the liquid eyeliner licking the top of my lid, ticklish. It's hard not to scrunch my eye up.

"I use my pinky to kind of balance my hand against my cheek, so I'm not so shaky as I run the liner along the lid. And you want to try to get as close as you can to the lashes."

I don't think I've been this close to Lelia before. She smells like stage makeup, of course, and hair spray, but there's a softer smell as well. Lilacs.

"Hey, do you want to be kind of silvery, like Ariel?" she asks, leaning back a little.

I shrug without opening my eyes. "Sure."

I hear her rummaging around in her own tool-box, and then I feel Lelia painting my face with a soft brush, like an artist on a canvas. When I was a little girl, Dad would always do my makeup for me if I was in a show. Now he or the other actors give me pointers.

"Almost finished! Just a little mascara," Lelia murmurs. "You don't need a lash curler because your lashes are so thick and long. You're lucky!" I feel myself blushing again under the makeup. "And wow, look at yourself! You look great."

I open my eyes and turn back to face the mirror. I've been totally transformed. I look a little like Lelia—the same silvery eye shadow sweeping up to my brows, the same glitter around my cheeks. A younger—geekier—version of ARIEL.

"Beautiful!" Lelia gives me her brightest smile. "You look beautiful!"

Now I give myself a smirk. I don't know what to do with compliments. I don't live for them the way Stella does. And I know Lelia is just trying to be nice. I know I'm not beautiful like my sister.

Stella is light and fair, thin and curvy all at once. (Just like Mom used to look in old photos.) Wherever we go, people do a double take when they see Stella. I hate to admit it, but she'd definitely make a great movie star. (She wants to go to Hollywood, not Broadway.) She's got the stuff. Star quality. *Stella* does mean "star," after all, as she always likes to point out.

I am the opposite of golden Stella. I am small and dark, and even though I am almost thirteen, I am still flat as a pancake. I know I have kind of a funny face—

heart-shaped, with a wide, high forehead and a small, pointed chin. My eyes are big and green, and maybe a little too far apart.

"Bug eyes," Stella will say when she is playing the role of the Mean Sister.

I look more like Dad (except that Dad is really handsome, so maybe I'd look better as a guy), and like Dad I want to be a serious stage actor, not a frivolous movie star. I want to move to New York City, not Hollywood, when I grow up.

The problem is, it takes so very long to grow up.

"You have great cheekbones," Lelia says, still focused on me. "You're lucky. You'll age well."

"Well, that's a relief," I reply in a tone my dad would call "dry."

Lelia lets out a laugh. And for the first time, her high-pitched laugh doesn't annoy me. It actually makes me laugh too.

"Hey, you know what?" Lelia says, leaning in close as if to impart a secret.

"What?"

"My acting teacher in college told me something I'll never forget. She said that simply being *pretty*"—she waves a hand dismissively in the air—"is not the most important thing. Confidence! Attitude! Spark! These are the things that make a great actress."

"But being pretty doesn't hurt, right?" I glance sideways at Lelia in the mirror. The fact is, she isn't just pretty, she's drop-dead gorgeous.

"Well, maybe it's more important on TV or in the movies." Lelia shrugs. "But Cass has told me that you're really serious about the stage, right?"

I feel my heart start to beat a little faster. Dad was talking to Lelia about me?

"I only want to go onstage," I say in a solemn voice.

"That's really cool!" Lelia pauses. "Cass says you're a terrific little actress. A natural."

I gaze down at my hands. A great big wave of happiness surges through me.

"Hey, have you ever heard of Sarah Bernhardt?" I nod, but Lelia rushes on ahead. "She was an actress from a long time ago—like the 1800s. I studied about her in this theater history class I took in college. She's still considered to be one of the greatest actresses of all time! She was one of the first celebrities. She lived in Paris, and everybody was fascinated by her. But the thing was, she wasn't a great beauty. In fact, some people wrote that she was kind of ugly in person. She had a big nose and kind of frizzy hair, and she was really skinny, which people didn't like back then. Can you believe it?" She shakes her head. "A little meat on the bones—that's what was fashionable. I wish that's the way it was today!"

I shake my head along with Lelia, but I'm thinking that she doesn't have anything to worry about. She hardly has any meat on her bones as it is.

"Anyway, all that stuff—how she looked—it didn't matter. When Madame Sarah made an entrance, the audience was in total awe." She pauses for emphasis. "Madame Sarah totally commanded the stage."

"Madame Sarah?"

Lelia nods. "Madame Sarah. Also known as *la petite étoile*—'little star' in French." Lelia is gazing at herself in the mirror. "One critic claimed that when Madame Sarah performed, it was 'pure incandescence.'" Lelia sighs. "To be called pure light. Can you imagine?"

Now I look at myself in the mirror too.

"No, I can't," I reply (dry again).

"Be patient, Junebug. Your time will come, you'll see." She starts smoothing back her hair. "I was such a geek when I was a kid. You should have seen me. I had braces and glasses."

Now I'm watching Lelia in the mirror again. I can't imagine her with braces. Her teeth are perfectly straight and pearly white. I can't imagine her with glasses, either. Her eyes are sky blue.

"Your time will come," she repeats, and turns to give me the biggest smile.

And I feel myself smiling back. I don't understand it. I've spent three and a half weeks *not* liking Lelia. I've spent three and a half weeks ignoring her attempts to be nice to me. I've wanted to be completely loyal to Mom, of course. But maybe Lelia isn't so bad. Maybe Mom left for some other reason besides Lelia.

"Oh! My cue's coming up, I better hurry!" Lelia pops up from her chair and rushes for the door, but then pauses and glances back at me. "See you later, Madame Junebug." And then she's gone.

I turn toward my reflection again.

"Madame Junebug," I repeat.

the seagull

I.

Here's how I see it:

It's my first big Broadway audition, and Scott Stevens just happens to be my scene partner. As soon as we have finished our scene together, a deep silence falls over the rehearsal hall.

At last the director stands and begins to clap—slowly at first and then faster, louder. The other auditioning actors have no choice but to stand and clap as well.

"That performance was so believable, so real!" the director cries, his voice breaking with emotion. "You two were born to play these roles. You were born to work together!"

From that moment on, Scott and I are a famous

duo, performing all the great tragedies together. We are ROMEO and JULIET, of course, dying for love. We are HAMLET and OPHELIA; OTHELLO and DESDEMONA. (I still haven't read *Cymbeline* yet, so I don't know whether that play has a great tragic couple in it or not.)

HERE'S HOW IT IS:

Stella is the one on the rehearsal stage auditioning with Scott, not me. I can only sit in a chair and watch in silence. There are no roles for twelve- or even thirteen-year-olds in *The Seagull*. (*Alas, alack.*)

Stella is auditioning for the role of NINA, the ingénue, and she's overacting, if you ask me. She flings her arms into the air as she talks about longing to lead an interesting life, longing to go on the stage.

Scott is quieter, less dramatic—more *real*, I think. As TREPLEV he talks quietly but truthfully about his own longing—for NINA herself.

As I watch the scene, I know why Dad thinks Scott "will make it." Dad doesn't think that about all the actors who come through the Blue Moon, only the ones who have "that something extra, that spark." I know Dad meets with Scott in his spare time, gives him acting lessons. That's what he always does with actors he believes in.

Does Dad believe in me? I think so, but I've never actually asked.

He says you're a terrific little actress. A natural.

That's what Lelia said last night. My stomach gives a little flip-flop of delight.

Terrific. A natural.

I wish I had the chance to show what I could do now, in front of everyone. It's funny, I hate getting up in front of kids in my classes at school. I hate when I have to do an oral report, or something like that. But I love getting up onstage. I'd love the chance to audition for *The Seagull.*

"Good work. Thanks, you two," Dad calls at the end of the scene. He pauses a moment, tugging at his chin thoughtfully. "Now, let's try Lelia and Scott together in the same scene, from the top again. When you're ready."

Lelia rises from her chair and walks toward the stage. She moves gracefully, like a dancer, and her legs are long ballerina legs. She and Scott look good onstage.

He's so fair and she's so dark. They whisper together for a moment, and then they separate, move a few feet apart, their backs to each other. Several moments pass in silence, and then the audition begins.

Lelia goes through the exact same scene that Stella just did—the same lines—but the feeling is totally different.

Stella was *acting*.

Lelia is *being*.

The difference is crystal clear.

"D-d-did you know that Chekhov died exactly at the height of his powers?"

Thespis, of course, sitting in the row behind me.

I put a finger to my lips, even though it was only a whisper. Auditions are solemn, serious. I don't want to miss any of Lelia and Scott's scene together.

Plus, I don't want to admit that I don't actually know that much about Chekhov except that he wrote *The Seagull* and that he is one of Dad's favorite playwrights. I've been waiting for Dad to take the time to explain to me in his Explaining Voice what he likes about Chekhov, about this particular play (like he normally would), but he hasn't.

"Good, good!" Dad calls when the scene comes to an end.

Now Dad moves on to other scenes, other actors. Everyone takes turns trying on a different character, as if they're trying on different clothes. Some of the clothes fit, some don't.

Auditions take all morning as usual, and as usual they wear the actors out. Lunch is a quiet affair. Then everybody scatters, rabbits into their own little rabbit holes, waiting in solitude for Dad to make his final decisions, post the cast list in the Green Room.

Everybody likes to pretend that auditions are no big deal, but they are. One big competition. Sometimes when the cast list goes up there's anger, sometimes tears.

"A thick skin—that's what you need to be a serious actor, Junebug," Dad has told me more than once. "You need strength, perseverance. And above all, courage."

And I promise myself I will have all those things. I lie alone (having miraculously dodged Thespis after lunch) on the concrete floor of the costume room (my own private rabbit hole). The gold brocade and tiny mirrors of *Romeo and Juliet* shimmer above me, but what I'm really seeing is myself (an older version of myself) walking the streets of Broadway, a starving artist starving for my art. I go to every audition, and each time I am so very close to getting the role—so very close—but each time the lead ultimately goes to another young actor. Finally I have no money left, and I know I must leave my beloved city, but I go to one final audition, and that's when my big break comes.

"One day you're a nobody; the next day you're a star."

That's what Mimi has told me. It happened to a friend of hers. The girl was an understudy on Broadway and the star fell sick, so Mimi's friend took the stage at the very last minute and the critics raved.

"And she was somebody, just like that," Mimi said, and snapped her fingers. "Overnight she had agents and directors and producers banging down her door."

I snap my fingers.

Just like that.

A nobody one minute.

Snap.

A star the next.

Snap.

"Did you hear something?"

I stop snapping and listen.

A voice. Two voices.

"Nobody's here. I was looking for Simon to fix a tear in my costume, but he's not around."

That's Lelia.

"I was looking for the cast list."

That's Christopher.

"Not up yet?"

"Nope."

CHRISTOPHER LONG, *character actor who thinks he should be a leading man; tall and muscular with thick red hair and pale, freckled skin; complains a lot; has a whiny voice.*

"How was my audition?" Christopher asks now, whining a little. "Tell the truth."

In *The Tempest*, Christopher plays ANTONIO, which is total typecasting if you ask me because ANTONIO is a big whiner and an all-around icky guy.

"I thought it was a strong audition," Lelia answers, and I wonder if she's really telling the truth. I thought Christopher was too stiff. "Very strong."

"Thanks." A pause. "And you were great, of course."

I'm about to roll out from under the costumes,

make my presence known. I might even tell Lelia that I thought she was great too.

"I'm sure you'll get Nina," Christopher says, his voice turning sly.

For some reason, the change in tone makes me freeze.

"Methinks you have Cass wrapped around your little finger."

I catch my breath and listen. Lelia says something, but it's too soft for me to hear.

"Oh, don't deny it!" Christopher cries, and then he's laughing, and he sounds like an old black crow.

Caw-caw-caw.

Again I miss what Lelia says. But then she's laughing too. The high-pitched laugh. Like a horse whinnying.

Whinny-whinny.

I lie perfectly still, waiting to hear what they'll say next.

"And what do you think of this place, anyway? Pretty rustic, huh? When I took the job I didn't know how boondocks it really was, did you?"

I wait for Lelia to defend the Blue Moon.

"Yeah, it's kind of the middle of nowhere," Lelia says.

Christopher must whisper something, because they both start laughing.

Whinny-whinny, caw-caw.

And then the voices fade. They must be heading to the Green Room to wait for the cast list.

I lie perfectly still, staring up at the costumes above me.

The knot is back inside my belly.

Wrapped around your little finger.

Is that true?

Does Lelia really have Dad wrapped around her little finger? Is that why he looks at her the way he does—as if he's forgotten his lines? Is that why Mom left?

Wrapped around your little finger.

And what about me?

Is that why Lelia was extra nice to me last night, helping me with my makeup, telling me about Madame Sarah, telling me my time would come and how Dad said I was a terrific little actress, a natural?

Did he even say that to her at all?

Wrapped around your little finger.

Maybe that's what Lelia does. Wrap people around her finger.

But why?

To get what she wants, I guess. All the best parts, all the attention.

All the director's attention.

I think about her audition this morning. How believable she was as NINA, how perfect in her role as a girl who longs for something exciting to happen in her life.

Lelia is an actress. A really good one.

For the very first time in my life, I wonder how you're supposed to know when the acting stops and the real person begins.

II.

HERE'S HOW I SEE IT:

```
                JUNEBUG'S PREVIOUS LIFE

                      ACT I

        SCENE I

        [A  single  spotlight  illuminates  this
```

scene—obviously a flashback to a quiet
Sunday morning exactly one year before.
Mom and daughter lie side by side among
the pillows of a large four-poster bed.]

MOM: Ah, a Free Sunday at last! No
rehearsals, no tech calls. No meals to
cook for the actors. Free at last!

JUNEBUG: I don't like Free Sundays,
because the Blue Moon is so empty.
Everyone either stays in their room or
leaves for the day. It's like a ghost
town.

MOM: Yippee! The lunatics have fled the
asylum!

JUNEBUG: Mom, actors aren't lunatics.

MOM: Well sometimes they act like
lunatics—you have to admit.

JUNEBUG: Maybe I'm a lunatic.

MOM: [smiling and wrapping her arms
around her child] Maybe you are, Junebug.
But you're my favorite lunatic. Anyway,
I'm glad for Free Sundays because it's

```
a time just for us, a time just for
family.
```

```
[The spotlight fades. The stage goes
black.]
```

HERE'S HOW IT IS:

The first Free Sunday of the Blue Moon season, but it's not a time just for family anymore, because there is no family.

At least not all together.

Mom and Beck aren't here.

And Dad isn't here either. He headed for the office right after breakfast, said he'd be doing paperwork and running lines all day. (He cast himself as TRIGORIN, another big role, in *The Seagull*, which is kind of weird because he usually only acts in one play a season.)

He doesn't ask me if I wanted to help him run lines.

Stella didn't ask me either.

"I'm running lines with Scott," she informs me, flashing a superior little smile, once she'd actually made it out of bed.

"But why are you running lines with Scott?"

"He asked me to." Stella keeps smiling.

"But a lot of his scenes are with Nina."

"Yeah, but I think Dad will be running lines with Nina," Stella says.

The knot is back, tight as a fist.

Lelia was given the role of NINA, of course. And as TRIGORIN, Dad falls in love with NINA onstage.

Wrapped around your little finger.

I gaze up into Stella's face for a moment. Should I ask her about Lelia?

"I hate my role," Stella says, pouting. "Masha is so boring." She disappears back into her room, closing the door behind her.

"At least you have a role," I whisper.

The tears are welling up. Again. I feel like such a crybaby lately. I hate Free Sundays. I don't want to be alone.

Suddenly I wonder what Thespis is doing today, right this very minute. Does his family go to church together like other families do around here? Do they eat dinner together? Do his mom and dad sit around and listen to Thespis rattle off information and exclaim over how brilliant their son is?

The image of Thespis—of anyone—being surrounded by loving parents is more than I can bear.

And so I head out the door and across the field. I miss Mom, and I'm going to tell her how much I miss her, how much I want her back.

At the start of the summer, when she left, she gave each of us a choice.

Beck, Stella, me.

She told each of us we could choose for the summer: the theater or the farm.

Beck chose to go with Mom, but Stella and I chose to stay.

Mom didn't seem all that surprised by our choices. She called me her little Junebug and told me I could change my mind anytime I wanted.

The thing is, I couldn't imagine a summer without the Blue Moon.

But I can't really imagine a summer without Mom, either.

As I come through the last field, I find Beck in overalls working on Mama Duvall's old red tractor, his arms and face streaked with dirt and oil.

BECKET HARLAN CANTRELL, *seventeen years old; dark brown hair and deeply tanned; total opposite of his sister Stella; laid-back, good-natured; prefers farming to the stage.*

"Hey, Beck."

Beck jumps back, banging his head on the open top of the tractor.

"Junebug!" He rubs the top of his head but grins at me anyway. "Mom said to keep a lookout for you. She knew you'd be lonely."

"I'm not lonely!" I scoff, even though that's exactly what I am.

"Well, we've been lonely for you! It's so quiet without our two drama queens."

"Stella is the drama queen, not me."

"Okay, whatever you say." Beck leans his back against the tractor. "Anyway, how's it going over there? Full houses every night?"

My chin goes up. I know Beck is just teasing. There are never full houses anymore. "We had fifty people last night!" I announce.

Beck squints off into the distance. "I remember when there were *two hundred and fifty* every night."

Now I squint too, but I can't see what Beck sees. I've never known what it's like to have full houses every night, like in the old days.

Simon has told me about it, though. He's told me how in the beginning the whole town would come out again and again, and folks would travel from miles around, just to see a show.

"Magic," Simon has said. "It was like your dad truly was Prospero, creating magic in the middle of nowhere."

I give Beck a nudge. "You could come see a show, you know, it wouldn't kill you."

"Arrrgggh, Shakespeare, arrrrgh!" Beck puts his hands around his neck, pretending he's being strangled.

I just have to laugh. "It's amazing you don't go onstage anymore. You're such a ham."

"No way," Beck says, shaking his head and going back to the motor. "No more drama for me."

I don't know when Beck became a farmer instead of an actor. It happened slowly. Even before the split, he'd stopped acting in plays and spent a lot of time with Grandma, learning how to bale hay and cut tobacco. He can fix any kind of machine, like this old tractor.

"*The Tempest* is not that bad," I inform him, stepping up onto the wheel, watching as he loosens a bolt. "Even *you* could figure it out."

"Oh, you think so, little sis?" Beck laughs. He bangs on the motor some, and then he glances sideways. "You doing okay, Junebug? Anything you want to talk about?"

I study a rusted patch on the top of the tractor. Beck is the first person to actually ask me if I want to talk. And part of me does want to talk, to somebody. But if I talk to Beck, wouldn't that be taking sides somehow? Against Dad?

"I'm okay. Everything's fine." I make my voice even, strong.

See? I'm a great actress too. A natural.

"Okay, Junebug." Beck leans his shoulder into me, and I lean back. "But let me know if you need anything, okay?"

I nod my head. My throat feels tight.

"Mama Duvall's still at church, but she'll be back soon. She already made the banana pudding!"

"Yum!"

I jump off the tractor tire and head up the driveway.

Mama Duvall's place is an old white farmhouse with a giant wraparound porch and great big windows like eyes looking out over the surrounding fields. Inside it's always dark and cool in the summer, and the whole house smells like the bread Mama Duvall is always baking and the strong coffee she always keeps going.

Slowly I take the grand staircase, one step at a time, to Mom's old room on the second floor. As I get closer to the top I start to get a strange fluttering in the pit of my stomach, like I've got butterflies.

I tiptoe to the open door of Mom's bedroom and I see Betty before I see Mom.

Betty is Mom's sewing dummy. She used to be my playmate when I was little. She would come to my tea parties and I would dress her up in costumes.

Now Betty is wearing a huge, frothy white wedding dress, and Mom is on the floor, working on the hem.

I've missed Mom so much. I'd planned to run and tackle her, the way Thespis's mom tackled him on that first day. But now something holds me back. I stay quiet, watching as she works.

EVALINE DUVALL CANTRELL, *middle-aged; in old photos looks just like her daughter Stella—blond and thin and gorgeous; now she's kind of spread out, like Mama Duvall, fuller; hair is darker at the roots and has streaks of gray running through it.*

As I study Mom from behind, I think about Lelia with her tiny waist and perfect skin and her thick dark hair like silk. I know she's a lot younger than Mom.

Does Dad love Lelia now because she's slim and young and doesn't have any gray hair? Does he not love Mom anymore because she doesn't look like she did in old photos?

It seems really awful not to love somebody just because they don't look like they used to in old photos.

Dad doesn't look like he used to in old photos either. His hair has a whole lot of salt with the pepper. And his face has wrinkles now, especially around the eyes and mouth. But he's still thin as a rail (as Mama Duvall says), and he still has a killer smile (as Mom used to say).

Would Dad love Mom again if she changed back to the way she was?

"Mom, maybe you should dye your hair."

Mom lets out a little gasp and whirls around.

"Junebug! You scared me half to death! I didn't

hear you come in." She reaches a hand up to her head. "What's this about my hair?"

"Have you ever thought of dyeing it?"

Mom cocks her head. She gazes across the room at me, wrinkling her brow, like I am a puzzle she's trying to figure out.

"And why do you think I should dye my hair?"

I look down at my feet.

"Um, because it's turning gray."

"A little gray never hurt anybody."

"But it makes you look old."

"Well, it's nice to see you, too, Junebug."

Mom's voice goes flat. She turns back to her sewing. I know I've hurt her feelings, but I can't say I'm sorry. I can't say anything at all.

So I just go and stand next to Betty, running my fingers lightly over the frothy material.

"Will you please hand me some more pins, Junebug?" Mom says after a while.

I find the pincushion and hand out the pins one by one.

"It's a really pretty dress, Mom," I whisper.

"Thanks, Junebug. I have three of these to finish

by the Fourth of July. Can you believe it?"

This is what Mom does during the rest of the year when the Blue Moon is closed. She makes wedding dresses for people from all over. I guess she's doing it full-time now.

"How's Simon?" Mom asks as she pins.

"He's seeing blue for *The Seagull*," I tell her. "Ocean blue." Simon always has color themes for the plays.

"Hmmmm." Mom nods thoughtfully. "And Stella. Is she behaving herself?"

"She's completely gaga over Scott Stevens."

"He's the young one, right? The cute one?"

"He's the one Dad thinks has real potential," I announce knowingly, as if the cuteness isn't what's important about Scott. "Anyway, she's running lines with him today. All day, she told me." I roll my eyes, even though that's exactly what I would love to do— run lines with Scott all day. "And she's being totally lazy. She won't do a thing."

Mom stops what she's doing and leans back on her heels, her blue eyes focused on me, really listening. I feel something releasing.

"Stella just acts like she's so above everything now.

She refuses to help with Breakfast and Office Duty, even though we're supposed to take turns. I can't get her to do anything at all."

"Did you talk to your father about it?"

Your father. I've never heard Mom say *"your father"* until this summer.

I shake my head. How can I tell her that I don't talk to Dad about much of anything lately?

"Well, I'll have a chat with Stella." Mom reaches out and smoothes back my hair. "I'll tell her she needs to do her part, okay?"

"Okay."

Now things feel the way they should, so I start rattling on about the Blue Moon as Mom goes back to her hemming. I talk about how *The Tempest* is actually starting to hum by night and how rehearsals for *The Seagull* are going by day. (A juggling act, as Dad always says, that's what summerstock is. You have to keep all the balls in the air and not let them hit the ground.) Finally I talk about how Stella is pouting over being MASHA.

"She'd rather be Nina, of course, because Nina's the beautiful one, the one everyone falls in love with, but Lelia is really perfect for Nina—" I stop short. I can't believe I said Lelia's name in front of Mom. I can't believe I'm actually talking about how perfect Lelia is when I've gone back to not liking her.

Wrapped around your little finger.

The words make my skin crawl.

"And your father, he cast himself as Trigorin, hmmm?" Mom asks, her voice strangely quiet, her hands still working with the hem.

I don't answer right away. I wonder if Mom has read the play, if she knows that TRIGORIN falls in love with NINA.

"Well, we're short on men this year." I know I'm just repeating something I heard Dad say. "Christopher isn't strong enough, he's too . . . stiff and whiny."

"Mmmm." Mom has a faraway look. "*The Seagull* is your father's favorite play—at least his favorite that Shakespeare didn't write."

"I know."

Mom stops what she's doing and searches my face. "What about you? Do you like *The Seagull*?"

"Yeah," I answer automatically, even though the truth is, I haven't read the whole play. And I haven't actually sat through every rehearsal, because I've been busy with all my other duties. So I don't really know if I like it or not. But if it's Dad's favorite play, it has to be great.

"I didn't want your father to do *The Seagull*," Mom says, almost to herself. "I think he should do plays that people around here can understand."

"But *The Seagull* is Real Theater," I say importantly.

Mom laughs and shakes her head. "You're so much like your father."

I turn away slightly. It should be a compliment, but for some reason it doesn't exactly feel like one.

And that's when something tugs at my brain. A scene from last year, at the end of the season. An argument.

Mom was talking about how the Blue Moon should do comedies.

"Plays that make people feel good," she said.

And Dad responded with his usual, that Real Theater is about more than just making people feel good, it's about making people think.

"Well, maybe people don't want to think all the time," Mom said. "Maybe they just want to be entertained."

"Real Theater!" Dad said back. "That's my goal. Bringing Real Theater to the masses."

"Don't you think that's a little arrogant, Cass? I mean, is it really your job to bring Real Theater to the masses? Maybe you should think about your audience a little more and your own ego a little less."

There was silence after that.

A terrible silence.

I mean, it's not like Mom and Dad never ever fought. They did fight. Sometimes they'd yell and slam doors. But they'd always make up.

Now as I replay the scene inside my head I remember waiting in the terrible silence, waiting for the yelling and the slamming of a door. But it never came.

And when I really think about it, neither did the making up.

"I hear you have a new addition to the company," Mom says.

It takes me a few minutes to come back to the here and now, to realize that Mom's talking about Thespis. He's the last person I want to discuss at the moment.

"He sounds like a nice boy . . . ," Mom begins.

"He's weird," I mumble.

"Weird? What do you mean?"

"Well, he lines things up, for one thing. He organizes all the breakfast stuff in a line."

"Maybe he's just very . . . linear."

"And he stutters. Don't you think that's weird? For somebody who is supposed to be 'quite the young thespian'?"

"Who called him that?"

"Dad. And he knows all this really obscure stuff about history. Theater history."

"Sounds like someone I know," Mom singsongs.

It takes me a few confused seconds to realize she's talking about me!

"You think I'm weird? Great, Mom, thanks."

Mom reaches out and tugs at my arm. "No, of course I don't think you're weird, honey pie. But it sounds like you two have a lot in common. Two peas in a pod."

"I am not a pea."

"And it's nice for you to have a friend, someone your own age."

"Why does everyone keep saying that?" I fume. "I don't like kids my own age."

"Oh, Junebug, it would help if you made more of an effort."

"Why?"

"You don't want to grow up too fast."

"Maybe I do."

Mom sighs, but doesn't say anything. She finishes the hem and then stands up to observe her creation, rubbing at the muscles along her lower back.

The dress is extra fancy, like a big white cake with lots of frosting. Mom never makes simple wedding dresses. They're always really ornate, which is kind of funny if you stop to think about it, because when Mom got married, she didn't even wear a wedding dress. Dad proposed, and they went to the courthouse that very day and a judge married them. Mom and Dad both wore jeans, and Mom had daisies woven into her long blond hair because they had been walking through a field when Dad asked her.

"Perfectly spontaneous!" Dad used to say when they'd tell the story of how they got married.

Dad loves the word "spontaneous." He uses it all the time when he's directing a new play or giving notes for the old play.

"Keep it spontaneous! Keep it fresh!" he'll say. "Even when you're doing the same play night after night, go for the unexpected."

Is that what Lelia is for Dad? A way to keep it spontaneous?

The thought makes me so sad, I want to cry. I keep staring at the dress, blinking back the sudden tears, and that's when another thought pops into my head.

Maybe Mom didn't want to go to the courthouse when she and Dad got married. Maybe she would have preferred something not so spontaneous. A big fancy wedding with a big fancy dress.

I rush to Mom and throw my arms around her.

"Junebug!" Mom cries in surprise. And then she wraps her arms around me.

It feels so good—wrapped in Mom's big arms. Maybe it wouldn't feel the same if she were skinnier.

"Mom?"

"Yes, sweetie pie?"

"You don't have to dye your hair."

"Thanks, Junebug, that's a relief."

III.

HERE'S HOW I SEE IT:

Now that I know what Lelia is really and truly like, I keep my distance. I tell myself I will never again be wrapped around anybody's little finger.

HERE'S HOW IT IS:

"Hey, Junebug, I have something for you!"

Lelia plops down in the chair beside me right before morning rehearsal is set to begin and holds something out to me.

"I had my roommate in New York overnight it to me. I thought I still had a copy of this from school."

It's a book. The cover is torn along one edge and shows a faded drawing of a girl with flowers in her hair.

Madame Sarah.

"It's kind of old, but it's the most comprehensive biography about her. It has pictures and everything." Lelia leans her shoulder into mine. I pull away slightly, but Lelia doesn't notice. She's flipping through the pages. I can smell lilacs again.

"There, see?" Lelia finds the photo section and holds it open for me.

The pictures are in black and white. One shows a woman with frizzy hair and (yes) a big nose, her face turned upward, her pale arms reaching for the sky.

One of her finest roles, Phèdre in Racine's classic, the caption reads.

"She was pretty eccentric," Lelia continues, flipping to another photo. "See? Here's a picture of her in her famous coffin."

"You mean there's a picture of her dead?"

"No, no!" Lelia's laugh whinnies out. "She kept a coffin in her dressing room, and she would lie in it before a performance. She had terrible stage fright—she would get physically sick—and it calmed her nerves, lying in a coffin, for some reason." Lelia makes a face. "Isn't that weird?"

I nod wordlessly, flipping through the pages myself. In a few photos Madame Sarah is dressed like a man, and I wonder if that means she played men's roles, which is funny when you stop to think about it, because in the really old days of theater, only men could play women's roles. (I know this without

Thespis telling me, thank you very much.)

"Five minutes," Coleman's voice calls out.

The other actors are flooding the room. It's nearly time for rehearsal to begin.

"Well, I just thought you'd like to borrow the book," Lelia says, with a shrug and a smile.

"Thanks."

"You're welcome." Lelia nudges my shoulder like we have a secret we're sharing. "Madame Junebug."

The knot is back.

Am I being wrapped again?

I don't know. But I like the book. It's pretty cool.

"Oh, there you are, Junebug."

Now it's Dad, in Roadrunner mode, coming to a skidding stop beside me.

"How now, Daddy-o?" I ask. I've hardly seen him at all. He wasn't home when I got back from Mama Duvall's last night. And he looks like he hasn't slept much. There are dark circles under his green eyes.

Plenty of time to rest in the grave!

"I know you were planning to do the Props for this show, as usual. . . ." Dad leans down to my level.

"Sure." I shrug like it's no big deal, but it is. I like

when Dad asks me to do Props, because it means I'm good at it. He wouldn't ask me otherwise.

"But I was thinking. . . . For this show . . . perhaps we could let our new intern have a go."

The knot tightens.

Have a go?

Thespis appears then, panting a little. He must have been trying to keep up with the Roadrunner.

"But . . . but . . . he's never done Props before." I find my voice at last.

"Of course he'll need you to give him some pointers, Junebug, but I'm confident this bright young man is up to the challenge. What do you say?"

I don't say anything. But it doesn't matter.

"Good, then, it's settled!" Dad pops back up and pats the top of my head.

"Woof, woof," I mumble.

"All right, people, let's get this show on the road," Dad calls, clapping his hands together. "From the top!"

I can feel Thespis standing beside me. I want to get up and push past him, make a beeline to the Costume Room. I want to lie on the floor and stare up at all that golden brocade from *Romeo and Juliet* and maybe then I'll feel better, maybe then I won't bawl like a baby.

But I can't seem to move. All at once my arms and legs are so heavy, like I'm weighted to the chair the way we weight the mask flats to the floor backstage, with concrete blocks.

Thespis takes a seat in the row behind me. I'm glad he can't see my face. And I'm glad Coleman just called "Places" so that all the actors are busy getting ready to begin *The Seagull*.

I shut my eyes tight. I tell myself that as soon as rehearsal is underway, I will make my own fast exit.

"Lights up," Coleman calls, even though it's just a formality. The lights don't really "go up" during rehearsal. They won't go up until the play is actually on the real stage.

There's a pause, and then MASHA/Stella speaks the first line of the play.

"'I am in mourning for my life.'"

I open my eyes.

I've watched rehearsal before, but I've never really heard the opening line. I've never really *listened*.

"'I am in mourning for my life.'"

The line is repeated, and it's like the words were written just for me.

I am in mourning for my life.

The words describe everything—this whole summer—so perfectly. Mom and Dad not living together. The family split in half. Dad not acting like himself, not talking to me about anything important. Lelia wrapping us all around her little finger. Thespis appearing out of the blue and making me feel dispensable, invisible.

I am in mourning for my life.

Everything about my life has changed this summer. Nothing is the way it used to be.

And I don't like it. Not one little bit.

"D-d-do you know why Chekhov called *The Seagull* a c-comedy when it has a tragic ending?"

"Do you know something?" I whirl around to face my shadow/my replacement. The concrete blocks have rolled away. My voice is a quiet hiss. "I don't care."

And now I make a fast exit. Before Thespis—or anyone else—can see me cry.

IV.

HERE'S HOW I SEE IT:

A terrible wailing fills the air. A sound so sorrowful it could break your heart.

The mother gently lays the baby in a basket, soft with blankets, and slides the basket under a row of glittering costumes.

Instantly the baby is soothed. The wailing stops. The tears fall away.

HERE'S HOW IT IS:

I lie with my back flat against the cool concrete floor, staring up at the golden brocade above me, the tiny, shimmering mirrors, waiting to be soothed.

The tears are still falling. Silent tears. But tears just the same.

For once, not even *Romeo and Juliet* can make it all better.

"'I am in mourning for my life.'"

I whisper the words, and that's what actually makes the tears start to slow down.

"'I am in mourning for my life.'"

Just saying the line makes me feel stronger some-how. And then I get an idea.

If I'm going to be in mourning for my life, I need to find the right costume.

I think through my clothes at home, but other than a black wool skirt and a long-sleeved black corduroy blouse, I can't think of anything in my closet that's actually 100 percent black.

And so I roll out from under the costumes, wipe my face with the back of my hand, and start looking through the racks.

"What are you looking for, *dahling*?" Simon inquires once he returns from wherever he was when I first arrived.

"Something black," I answer without turning around, so he can't see my puffy eyes.

"Is there a funeral I don't know about?"

"Yes, mine." A pregnant pause, and then I try the line out on an audience: "'I am in mourning for my life.'"

"Ah, I see."

Simon puts a finger to his lips, thoughtful for a moment, and then begins to help in the search.

"Hmmm . . . the black shift from *Medea* would be

too hot, I'm afraid, and there are several maid costumes, of course, but I think they would all just swallow you whole. And the black toga from *Prometheus* would just look like a sack on you. . . ." He tut-tuts, hands on hips. "Well, there's nothing for it. I'll just have to create something new, just for you!" He whirls around and heads for the sewing room.

I hurry to follow. Simon whips out his tape measure.

"You're getting taller."

"I am?" I glance into the full-length mirror. I don't think I look any taller. In fact, I think I still look like such a baby. A baby with big, puffy, crybaby eyes.

Simon nods. "My *dahling* June is growing up."

"I wish."

Simon gets the tea ready and I sit and sip while he unfurls a bolt of black cotton across the sewing table.

"Thin and light—perfect."

The scissors flash. Simon never hesitates while he works. He never uses a pattern.

"I see it all in my head," he's told me before. "It's just . . . there!"

Mom is the same way. Watching her begin a new dress is like watching a magician at work.

In no time at all, Simon has made me a perfect little black dress. Sleeveless, simple, light as air. I slip it on and whirl around in front of the mirror.

"Brilliant, *dahling*," Simon breathes, making a few final adjustments. "If I do say so myself. You look *mahvelous*."

"I love it, Simon! Thank you!" The tears are coming again, and I'm not sure I'm strong enough to stop the flood, so I throw myself at Simon and hold on tight.

"Goodness! It's always nice to be appreciated, *dahling*!" Simon exclaims, laughing, but when I don't let go, the laughing stops, and slowly his arms wrap themselves around me.

We stand that way for a long, long time.

"I know it hasn't been easy, my dear, sweet girl," Simon whispers. "But I truly believe things will turn out right in the end. You'll see."

I nod my head up and down. I want to believe Simon. Maybe he's seen something in his tea leaves after all. But I'm not sure that I do.

V.

HERE'S HOW I SEE IT:

Years from now, the patrons who were lucky enough to be present during the final performance of *The Tempest* at the Blue Moon Playhouse will recall how the now famous Madame Junebug amazed the crowd with her ability to *be* Thunder.

"The storm was so real!" one fan exclaims. "It gave me shivers!"

"I wanted to run for cover, the thunder was so terrifying!" another pipes up.

"I couldn't believe my ears. I've never been more frightened in all my born days!" yet another devoted fan gushes.

HERE'S HOW IT IS:

Nobody in the audience knows I'm Thunder (I'm not in the program), but I make the most of my final performance anyway.

I beat my fists as hard as I can against the sheet of tin. I drum my fingers up and down, lost in the rhythm of the storm.

Coleman actually lets me go on a few extra minutes before signaling me to cut the storm.

I hide out in the Costume Room for most of the show. Thespis is doing a fine job as Gofer now. ("He picks things up so quickly," I heard Dad say.) But as the play ends, I hurry to the wings to listen to Dad's voice, his final speech as PROSPERO.

And then it's "Blackout!" for good on *The Tempest*. The actors rush to take their bows.

"Off with my head!" Ray leans over so I can help remove the beastie for the very last time. "Methinks I'll be happy to be rid of old Caliban."

"'O brave monster!'" I hug the beastie close. "I will protect thee by giving you a place of honor in the Prop Room!"

"Down with the old, up with the new!" a voice bellows.

Enter George, our Technical Director (aka TD).

GEORGE McHALE, *a teddy bear of a man—big and loud; gruff, but sweet as can be.*

"Are you ready for Strike Night, me maties?" George makes his voice sound like a pirate.

"Aye-aye, Captain," I reply.

"D-d-do you know why it's called Strike?" Thespis asks, a shadow behind me.

I slip the beastie over my head and turn to face him. It's pretty obvious I've been avoiding Thespis over the past few days. I know I should apologize for hissing, but I can't.

"Okay, why is it called Strike?" I ask. Maybe I can't apologize, but I'll try to at least be nicer.

Thespis shrugs.

"What, you mean you don't know?" I cock my beastie head to one side, and it almost tumbles to the ground.

Thespis shrugs again.

"Okay, Strike Night. Well, I guess it's because we *strike* it all down—the old set," I explain, my voice echoing inside the mask. "And then we build the new one. All in one night."

"You mean you stay up the whole n-n-night?"

"Yeah."

"Until the sun c-c-comes up?"

"Yeah."

"Until the b-b-birds start singing?"

"I guess."

"Wow, that's pretty c-c-cool. I've never stayed up all night before."

"Neither has June*bug*," Stella says as she happens by. Perfect timing to embarrass me, like always. "She usually falls asleep after midnight, just like a little baby."

"Well, you snore!" I call after her, tired of being the one who's always in the embarrassed seat. "Like a buzz saw!"

"Yeah, right," Stella calls nonchalantly back over her shoulder.

"You do," I mutter, but it doesn't matter.

Scott isn't around anyway, and I doubt Thespis cares whether Stella snores or not.

"Okay, people, let's get to work!" George's voice booms out. He breaks everybody into Crews, as usual, so Strike will go faster.

Thespis and I get Props Crew, of course, since I'm supposed to "show him the ropes" so he can replace me in the next show. I'm still not happy about it, but I decide to go as quickly as I can so the whole thing will be over sooner.

Together we gather up *The Tempest* Props for the very last time. We put all the weapons back in the Prop

Room, and I make sure the beastie is comfortable on a high shelf.

"Anon, brave monster," I murmur. "I won't forget thee."

Now we take the goblets and bottles to the kitchen to give them a good sudsing before storing them away for future use.

On the way I happen to spy Lelia and Christopher hanging out near the actors' lounge, whispering and laughing together.

Whinny-whinny, caw-caw.

I give them a hard stare, but they don't even notice.

A big rule at the Blue Moon: Strike Night is not a time for lounging about. Everybody (even the stars) is supposed to pitch in.

I wonder if Lelia wrapped somebody around her little finger (George? Dad?) so she doesn't have to work so hard tonight.

"You d-d-don't like her very much, d-d-do you?" Thespis asks once we're in the kitchen standing over the sink.

"Who?" I stop washing a goblet and turn to look at him.

"Lelia."

"What do you mean?"

"You always g-g-get this look when she's around."

"What look?"

"Your face gets kind of frozen."

I reach up and touch my face. Is it frozen? I don't know. I *do* know that the way Lelia makes me feel is all confused now, jumbled up.

I was certain I hated her at the start of the season, and then I wasn't so sure I hated her anymore, and I actually started to like her just the tiniest bit. And now I don't know what to feel about her.

"I d-don't like my stepdad very much either," Thespis says.

It takes a few seconds for the words to sink in, the meaning, and then something just snaps.

"She is *not* my stepmom!"

My heart starts to pound. A storm, with thunder and lightning.

"I thought—"

"I have a mom and I have a dad." I put my face close to Thespis so he has to look me straight in the eye for a change. "I do not have a *step* anything!"

I drop the goblet I'm holding into the sink so the soapy water splashes straight up like a fountain. And then I turn and exit the scene.

I don't care if I'm supposed to "show Thespis the ropes." I don't care if I'm supposed to "give him a chance." I don't want a know-it-all following me everywhere I go, spouting stupid information, thinking he knows something I don't even know about my own life.

In the dark I stand, a storm building, a storm of thunder and lightning. Should I go backstage and find Simon, ask him what's going on with Mom and Dad? Or should I head home? Not to Dad's home, which is always empty, but to Mom's new home at Mama Duvall's?

Maybe I made the wrong choice at the start of the summer. I couldn't imagine life without the Blue Moon. I thought Dad needed me more, but maybe I was wrong. He certainly found an understudy for me easily enough.

"Hey, June*bug*, give me a hand."

It's Stella, loaded down with a bundle of costumes. She dumps most of the pile into my arms without waiting for an answer and keeps going.

I'm tempted to drop the costumes on the ground and stalk away, but of course I don't.

You're a martyr. Dad's little theater slave.

Silently—still thunderous on the inside—I follow my sister to the Costume Room. I unload the bundle onto the sewing table and just stand, staring down at all the different colors of fabric, waiting for the storm to break.

"What're you doing standing there like a dress dummy?" Stella laughs. "Earth to bug brain! Don't you have a job to do?"

"I am not a bug brain. Stop calling me that."

"Well, then, *dahling*, if you need something to do—"

"It sounds really stupid when you say *dahling*."

"It sounds really stupid when you speak, period."

"Now, now, you two!"

Simon appears then, clapping his hands together for attention.

"Sisters should not bicker-bicker so. One day you will realize how precious it is to have a sister. I was an only child, you know, and all my life I've wished for a sibling. In fact, when I was a very young boy, I created an imaginary sister to be my companion so I wouldn't be so lonely."

I look at Stella.

Stella looks at me.

Methinks we're having the same thought: An imaginary sister might be better than a real one.

"My imaginary sister's name was Sabina," Simon continues in a wistful voice. "I told her all my secrets, all my fears. I was never lonely with Sabina."

"What happened to her?" I ask, glancing around. Maybe Sabina is still here.

"Well, *dahling*, one day I woke up and—*poof*—she was gone. I suppose I didn't need her anymore. I'd grown up." Simon sighs. And then he turns and raises an eyebrow at me and Stella. "I want you two to really make an effort. Be kind to each other."

Stella and I exchange doubtful glances as Simon heads out the door, but we start sorting through the costumes anyway.

Be kind to each other.

The thing is, it used to not be so hard.

Once upon a time Stella played the Nice Sister and I was her perfectly adoring little sidekick. She let me follow her around everywhere. She laughed at the "goofy" but "amusing" things I said. She always tried to make me feel better about being such a loser at school. But when she hit eighth grade, things seemed to change overnight. She closed her door a lot, wouldn't let me in. She said I was too young to hang out with her new friends. She still laughed at the "goofy" things I said, but she didn't call them "amusing" anymore, just "weird."

"You must be relieved—you don't have to do Props for the next show." Stella is the first to break the silence.

I want to shriek at her, the way she does at me sometimes.

No, I'm not relieved! I'm replaced!

But I have a feeling Stella's actually making an effort to *be kind*, so I will make an effort too.

"Do you have all your lines for *The Seagull*?" I ask. "I could help if you want."

"No, I'm okay." Stella shrugs. "It's not like I have that many, anyway."

And you have Scott. I want to say it, but I don't.

"I hate my costume," Stella continues, glancing around to make sure Simon is still gone. "I look terrible in black. It's not even a cool black. It's just plain cotton. Totally dull."

"Well, I doubt you really look terrible," I reply. I've never seen Stella look terrible in anything. Even when she was a donkey in a school play, she was a beautiful donkey. "But it's not like you should look really great, either. You're supposed to be in mourning for your life!"

"What a stupid line! I hate it."

"It's not stupid!"

"Nobody's in mourning for their whole life."

"A lot of people are!" I cry out, and I'm about to add *me, for one*, but I stop myself. "I think Masha is a cool part."

"I'd rather be Nina."

"I'd rather be *anything*."

"Yeah, I'd just die of boredom if I couldn't be onstage."

I know Stella's making an effort and everything, but still, she *has* to remember what it's like to be too young for roles. She's only been an ingénue for one season!

"Hey, what about your *boyfriend*?" Stella asks, giving me a little nudge.

"Boyfriend?"

"Trace. He must have a serious crush on you. He follows you around like a lovesick puppy."

I'm so shocked I can't form any words.

"But—but—but that's only because Dad said I had to show him the ropes," I splutter at last. "Which I hate doing, by the way."

"Well, Dad thinks he's something special. He sure spends enough time with him."

"Yeah, I know."

The knot is back.

"I guess he thinks he has potential, like Scott," Stella says.

Something snaps. Again.

"But he has a stutter!" I cry out. "How can he seriously want to go onstage?"

"He doesn't stutter all the time, and besides, who knows, maybe theater is good for people who stutter. Gives them confidence or something." Stella pauses. "Anyway, it must be nice to have him around—you're both such theater geeks. You must have a lot to talk about."

"I am *not* a theater geek, and no, it is *not* nice having him around! He's such a shadow, it drives me crazy. He's always there. He never leaves me alone! And he's such a know-it-all. Who's he trying to impress anyway with all his dumb, ancient information?"

"Junebug—" Stella tries to interrupt, but I'm on a roll.

"D-d-did you know this? D-d-did you know that?" I mimic Thespis's voice. "D-d-did you know you're being really annoying?"

"Junebug—" Stella starts again.

"And what's wrong with him, anyway? It's not just the stutter. It's like he's from another planet. He never looks you in the eye, and he's always lining things up—"

Stella kicks me in the shin.

"Ow, what'd you do that for?" I lean over to rub my leg.

Stella doesn't answer. She's not looking at me. She's staring down at a costume in her hands, and suddenly it's the most fascinating thing in the world.

And that's when I know.

I have an audience.

I put a hand over my mouth. As if that will do any good. The words are already out there. I can't take them back. I feel sick to my stomach, and all I want to do is disappear—*poof!* But I have to turn around first. I have to make myself turn around.

Thespis is standing just inside the doorway. He's gazing down at the floor, hair falling like a curtain, so I can't see his eyes, his face.

But I can see Simon's. He's there too. I can see the surprise, the disappointment.

My mouth opens, but nothing comes out. I don't know what to say.

Thespis nods his head a couple of times, like he's agreeing with something, and then he turns and disappears.

"I'm sorry," I whisper at last, eyes to Simon, pleading.

"June Olivia."

Simon's voice is strangely quiet—just like when Mom and Dad fought last year. And just like last year, I wish someone *would* yell.

"I'm not the one to whom you should apologize."

"I know, but—"

Simon waves a hand in the air, cutting me off. He moves a little closer, keeping his voice low.

"You asked what was *wrong* with Trace." Simon's left eyebrow goes way up. "There's nothing *wrong* with him. He has something called Asperger's Syndrome, if you must know. It means . . . well, it means that he sees things a little differently than others do, that he focuses on things in a rather intense way." Simon pauses. His voice and his eyebrow lower. "He's unique, different. I thought you, of all people, would be able to understand that."

I want to rush into Simon's arms like I did the other day, but something tells me not to. I want to hear the word "*dahling*," because I didn't hear it once in Simon's whole quiet speech.

Because I don't feel much like a *dahling*.

I feel like I'm going to be sick. I can't imagine actually telling Thespis I'm sorry. I can't imagine ever facing him again.

VI.

HERE'S HOW I SEE IT:

I rush to find Thespis and act out the perfect apology scene.

Thespis is so awed by my performance, he immediately forgives me.

Simon forgives me too, and I go back to being *dahling*, like always.

HERE'S HOW IT IS:

I slink away into the dark long before Strike is over, long before the sun comes up or the birds start singing.

At home I sit on the edge of Mom and Dad's empty bed, staring at the phone, willing it to ring. But it doesn't, and I'm afraid of calling Mom myself, waking her up.

And maybe I'm afraid of what she'll say.

I know she'll say that I have to apologize. And deep down I know it's what I must do. But I can't imagine actually doing it.

Back in my own room, in my own bed, I pull the sheet over my head.

O how I wish I could magically go back to the beginning of the night, "start at the top," as Dad says in rehearsal. I'd revise the script as I went along so I wouldn't end up the villain, a role I know I wasn't born to play.

In the morning, I head for Mama Duvall's so I can

avoid Thespis, avoid Simon (no *dahling*), but halfway there, I stop in my tracks.

The show must go on!

I know how much there is to do at the Blue Moon. Strike happens in one night, but the next day, there are still all the finishing touches to be done: the painting and the decorating of the set, the gathering of the Props, the last-minute costume changes, the light and sound checks.

The show must go on!

At the Blue Moon, everything's bustling already. Backstage it's like inside one of Mama Duvall's beehives. All the worker bees busily buzzing around, making honey.

I vow to apologize to Thespis as soon as I see him, but everybody's so busy, I get swept up in the buzzing. The whole day goes by in the blink of an eye, and I'm never actually alone with Thespis. He's a worker bee, darting here and there, making sure he has all the final Props ready for *The Seagull*. And then night falls and everybody's concentrated on Tech Rehearsal.

Do you know why it's called a Tech Rehearsal?

Because it's when you rehearse all the technical cues for the play—lights and sound.

The dialogue goes on inside my head.

Outside my head, Thespis isn't saying a word.

At least not to me.

He's Simon's shadow now, Simon's own personal theater encyclopedia. Simon reacts with awe to each and every tidbit. He even uses the *d* word.

I am in mourning for my life.

I don't say it out loud, but I don't have to.

VII.

HERE'S HOW I SEE IT:

Opening Night! I am waiting in the wings, preparing for my entrance. I am breathing deeply, from the very center of my soul. When the stage manager gives the cue, I step out from the wings. I am blinded for a moment, but I know the audience is out there, just beyond the glare. I can feel them. So many eyes, watching me.

I am waiting, waiting for the moment to speak the very first line of the play. . . .

HERE'S HOW IT IS:

"'I am in mourning for my life.'"

I whisper the words along with Stella. I listen to the tiny ripple of laughter. The words are meant to be funny because they are so melodramatic and MASHA/Stella says the line in such a deadpan way. And I actually see how the response from the audience brings a change over my sister.

Stage legs.

For once I am sitting at the very back of the house on Opening Night instead of backstage against the mask flats.

No thunder to roll in *The Seagull*.

No Props to care for.

No need to play Gofer, either.

Thespis is performing my roles perfectly.

"'I am in mourning for my life.'"

Stella says the line again and I close my eyes, listening to the many voices, the many characters.

Chekhov's words are so very different from Shakespeare's. (Of course, Shakespeare is really old English, and Chekhov is not-so-old English, but it's translated from Russian.) It's more than that, though.

In *The Seagull* not much happens, but the characters

talk and talk and talk. They talk about what makes them sad, and they talk about what makes them happy. One minute they're laughing with joy, the next minute they're crying with sorrow. They've all come together for a visit in this big summerhouse in the Russian countryside, and yet they can't seem to get along. There are tons of people around at all times, and yet every single person on the stage is lonely. And nobody loves the person they're *supposed* to love.

MASHA/Stella loves TREPLEV/Scott who loves NINA/Lelia who falls in love with TRIGORIN/Dad who is the boyfriend of ARKADINA/Mimi.

It's kind of confusing.

And real.

Watching all the characters yearn for someone they can't have makes all my own questions start whirling around inside my brain like a tornado.

Does Mom still love Dad?

Has Dad fallen in love with Lelia?

Does Lelia love Dad back, or does she simply want someone to wrap around her little finger?

What am I supposed to do? Whose side am I supposed to take?

What happens when the summer ends?

Bang!

A gunshot.

That's how *The Seagull* ends.

And even though I've sat through rehearsals, even though I knew what was coming, I nearly jump out of my seat along with everybody else. I feel the shock rippling through the audience.

And even though I know the gunshot wasn't really the young hero of the play, TREPLEV/Scott, killing himself, but actually George shooting a blank gun on cue in the wings, my heart aches along with the rest of the audience because the ending is so, so sad.

D-d-do you know why Chekhov called The Seagull a comedy when it has such a tragic ending?

Thespis asked me the question. And now I wish someone would tell me the answer.

alcestis

I.

HERE'S HOW I SEE IT:

Auditions are over. Preparations for a new show begin. I am given a script with my very own name written along the top cover. I set about marking all my lines with yellow highlighter—so very many lines!

"How will you memorize all those lines in such a short amount of time?" a cast mate asks.

"Well, if you must know, I have a photographic memory," I answer modestly. "I can read through the script once and know every single line—just like that."

"Amazing!" the cast mate cries in awe. "How lucky you are!"

HERE'S HOW IT IS:

I sit alone, against the wall of the rehearsal room, waiting for rehearsals to begin, staring down at my very own script for the next play. I haven't even bothered writing my name on the cover. I don't even need a yellow highlighter since I have no lines to highlight.

The new play is *Alcestis* by Euripides. Ancient Greek stuff, just like *Medea*, in which characters utter cool phrases like:

> O Zeus!
> O wicked fortune!
> O turning wheel of the sky!
> Such is the road most wretched I have
>   to walk!

At least most of the characters utter cool phrases like that. As for me, I will not be uttering one single word.

All summer I've known *Alcestis* is my one big chance to be a character, not just a sound effect; to be onstage instead of backstage.

All summer I've assumed Dad would merge the two

young characters in the play into one (just like he did with *Medea*), and I would be:

CHILD I, *firstborn of ADMETUS and ALCESTIS.*

I never even considered that Thespis might get that role, and that I would simply be:

CHILD II, *second-born of ADMETUS and ALCESTIS (silent character).*

Silent character!
The description blurs on the page of the script in front of me.
Silent character!
I feel sick.
I feel angry.
I feel betrayed.
Just like in Shakespeare.
In Shakespeare, characters are always being betrayed by those closest to them. In *The Tempest*, PROSPERO/ Dad was betrayed by his very own brother, ANTONIO/ Christopher, and banished to a deserted isle.

And now my own father has betrayed me by giving the only child speaking role to Thespis (aka my shadow, my replacement).

"D-d-did you know that in early Greek t-times, actors wore specific masks so the audience would always know immediately who the g-good guy was and who the villain was?"

Thespis has entered the scene. But he's not talking to me, of course. He's talking to Ray.

"Oh, yeah?" Ray says. "Now, that would be handy in real life, don't you think? If people wore certain masks to show if they were good or bad."

The words hit me—kind of like a punch in the stomach.

Which mask would I wear? Am I a good guy or a villain?

I don't know anymore.

In *Alcestis*, the villain is DEATH (Christopher got the role so it's typecasting again), and in the beginning DEATH is described as "hateful to mankind, loathed by the gods."

All at once that's exactly how I feel.

It's like he's from another planet.

The words—my words from Strike Night—are truly hateful.

The thing is, I remember overhearing a girl at school whisper those exact same words to another girl. About me. It was fourth grade, and I'd thought both girls were my friends.

Back then I cried and cried when I got home. And Dad took me in his arms and told me how special I was, how unique, and that I shouldn't ever care what other people think of me, but just always be myself.

But I did care. The words hurt.

And so I know the words must have hurt Thespis, too. So why can't I do the right thing and tell him I'm sorry?

"All right, folks, we're about to begin!"

Coleman doesn't use a megaphone, but her voice carries, loud and strong, anyway. The cast has slowly trickled into the rehearsal room and now they all immediately come to attention as Dad makes his grand entrance.

"Would you give your life so that the one you love might live?"

And what an opening line!

Chills run down my spine.

"That's the question Euripides is asking in our new

play, *Alcestis*." Dad continues. "An age-old question that gets to the very heart of duty, loyalty, love. The question transcends time and place. It's universal. It's simple. Would you give your life so that another might live?"

Dad scans his audience, waiting for the impact of his words to hit.

I get another chill.

The question is really scary. How would you even be able make that kind of decision?

Would I die for someone I loved? Would I die for Mom or Dad? Would I die for Beck or Stella?

Would any of them die for me?

I kind of doubt Stella would.

I glance over at my sister. She's sitting across the room, staring off into space, so I doubt she's even really listening to Dad. She hates when Dad goes on and on about stuff like this.

"*Boring!*" she'll say.

"Euripides was the first great playwright of the ancient era because he was the first to create real characters, not just the usual stereotypes of the hero and the villain, but complex characters, human beings *with flaws*." Dad pauses dramatically. "Flaws are what make a character interesting. Our flaws are what make *us* inter-esting."

Silence as Dad waits for his words to sink in.

Is that really true? Do flaws really make a person interesting?

I glance across the room again.

Stella looks perfect because she's so beautiful, but she's definitely flawed. She's vain and she can be mean and selfish. Does that make her interesting?

Scott is gorgeous *and* kind. Flawless, if you ask me. And yet he's totally interesting despite his utter per-fection.

Now my gaze falls on Lelia, and the knot is back.

Lelia seems perfect. She's beautiful and she doesn't seem vain or selfish or mean. She's always trying to be so nice to me. She's always looking at Dad as if he hung the moon. But is it only an act? Why would she talk about Dad behind his back if she loves him?

"The character of Admetus is flawed because he is a pillar of the community." Dad's Explaining Voice starts up again. "He is respected by everyone—a good friend, a good father, a loving husband. And yet when he is told by the gods that he must die, he cannot do it. In fact, he is so afraid of death he asks everyone he knows—his father, his mother, his friends, his wife—to die in his place. What kind of person would actually do that? Ask someone else to die in their place? What kind of person could live with himself after allowing another to die? After allowing *his own wife*, mother to his young children, to die so that he might live?"

Dad's face has changed. He is fierce, angry. Disgusted.

"A coward." Dad says the word as if he's spitting something out. "Only a coward would let his own beloved wife die for him. Admetus is a coward, and that's a terrible flaw."

Dad has been shifting his gaze from one actor to another during his speech, and now his eyes fall on me.

And it's like they're burning a hole right through me.

Dad must know what I did, what I said about Thespis. He must know that I haven't apologized either. He must know that I'm a coward. A terrible coward.

Maybe that's why he gave the speaking part to Thespis. Maybe that's why he made me a silent character. Because I don't deserve more.

"Okay." Dad claps his hands together, the lecture

before rehearsal over. He turns to the stage. "Time to get down to business. Let's start from the top."

I close my eyes.

O how I wish I could clap my hands together, and the summer would magically start over from the top—just like that.

II.

Here's how I see it:

The coffin was made especially for me, carved from the finest, smoothest mahogany and lined with the softest satin. When I lie down flat inside my very own coffin, all my fears, all my pain and anger melt away.

Here's how it is:

The coffin is propped on its side at the very back of the Prop Room. It is made of plain plywood, painted black. I have to drag it flat onto the floor and then I have to take a broom and a rag to get out all the cobwebs and dust.

I can't remember what play the coffin was used for,

but I know it hasn't been used for a long, long time.

I've brought some pillows from home and I found some extra satin in the costume room (while Simon was gone). I make my little bed and then I lie down and close my eyes.

I am the great Madame Sarah, and I am overcome with *le trac*. (That's French for "stage fright." I learned it from Lelia's book.) *Le trac* is blinding, paralyzing. The Stage Manager has called "Places" already. There are thousands of people in the theater. They've come to see me perform, and yet I'm not sure I'll even be able to go onstage. But as I lie flat in my coffin, eyes closed, a calmness overtakes me. A peacefulness. I know *le trac* will soon pass and I'll be able to do what I must do.

I open my eyes and stare at the Props hanging from the rafters overhead.

I've never really had *le trac*. Not here at the Blue Moon. Not before going onstage.

Dad has always joked that stage fright was the reason I was born in July instead of June, but the truth is, I've never known a moment's fear when I'm waiting in the wings to make an entrance.

It's real life that gives me stage fright.

The first day of school.

The next day of school.

Every single day after that until the last day of school.

Every single day of real life is like standing in the dark, waiting for a chance to get back into the light, waiting for a chance to get back into the magic of the Blue Moon.

But now it's like I'm in the deepest dark, even though it's the middle of the Blue Moon season, and I have the worse case of *le trac* ever.

Why can't I say I'm sorry to Thespis?

Why can't I talk to Simon?

Why can't I tell Dad how angry I am, how much I want things to be the way they used to be?

Why am I such a coward?

Why am I so very flawed?

III.

HERE'S HOW I SEE IT:

Like every serious actress I am able to cry on cue. When faced with Tragedy onstage, the tears pour down like rain. And the audience cries with me because they can truly *see* my pain, truly *feel* my sorrow.

HERE'S HOW IT IS:

"Tears, kids!" Dad calls when Thespis and I exit our one (and only) scene. "You're watching your own mother die before your very eyes. We'll need tears by Opening Night."

"Have you ever had to cry on cue before?" Lelia takes us under her wing during the break.

Thespis immediately shakes his head.

I think about all the tears I've being crying lately, but I guess those don't count. It's real life, not stage. So I shake my head too.

"Well, this is what you have to do." Lelia takes a deep breath. "As an actor, you must work on your character before rehearsal, you must prepare on your own. So while you're learning your lines"—Lelia glances at me—"or while you're learning your role," she adds quickly, "you need to work on that character's inner feelings. If the character cries onstage, you as the actor can use a sad memory from your past. A death in the family, even the death of a pet, something like that, something that's happened to you that brings you in touch with your own feelings of sorrow, of loss."

Lelia stops and glances from Thespis to me.

"Do you understand?"

Thespis nods.

I shrug like of-course-I-understand-I-was-practically-born-on-a stage-after-all-what's-the-big-deal?

Part of me is suddenly angry that Lelia is the one giving us this acting lesson instead of Dad, and yet another part of me wants desperately to hear what she'll say next.

"Now, what you want to do is concentrate on how you felt at that moment in your life when you lost something or someone dear to you. Here, I'll show you."

Lelia closes her eyes. She takes several deep breaths. And then she remains still for a few moments.

When she opens her eyes—*poof*—she's crying, just like that! Real tears. Streaming down her face.

Thespis immediately reaches into his pocket and holds out a Kleenex.

"Thanks!" Lelia dabs at the corners of her eyes, laughing a little. "See how easy it is? When you're onstage, use that specific memory, use those feelings of sorrow you've stirred up during your preparation. And then you'll be able to cry when you have to." She gives us both a big smile.

I think about Lelia's lesson for the rest of the day. It seems easy enough. There are so many things I'm sorrowful about right now, and the tears are always threatening anyway. Crying on cue should be easy.

But it's not.

Every time I'm onstage for rehearsal, I can't seem to focus on the scene. Instead I start thinking about what a coward I am because I can't apologize to Thespis. And I start thinking about what a disappointment I am to Simon. And then I start wondering if Dad knows everything and if he's punishing me by making me a silent character and not talking to me about anything.

And finally, as I watch Lelia going through her death scene, I start thinking about how weird it is that she is playing my mother onstage. What if she starts playing my mother offstage, too? What if I end up with a stepmother in real life? And so, by the time Lelia's actually dead at the end of the scene, I'm way beyond tears and somewhere closer to rage.

"Tears, kids, we'll need tears," Dad calls after another (tearless) rehearsal.

"You know, Junebug, you kind of look like you're smiling during your scene, not crying," Stella informs me during the break—in front of Scott, of course.

I don't even respond. What's the point?

"It's not easy to cry on cue," Scott says, giving me an encouraging, gorgeous smile. "And it's a small part so it's hard to find your motivation."

"There are no small parts, only small actors," I mumble—an automatic response.

Scott's blue eyes light up. "Hey, that's right, Junebug! What a great attitude to have!" He gives me a friendly nudge.

"Oh, she's just repeating something Dad always says." Stella rolls her eyes. "She's quite the little parrot, our June*bug*." Her voice is light, but I can tell she's miffed that I've (yet again) said something to impress Scott.

And impressing Scott almost makes everything better.

Almost.

IV.

HERE'S HOW I SEE IT:

My birthday is a national holiday.

All across the land there are parades through the streets.

All day long flowers and gifts from admirers around the world arrive at my door.

My friends throw a huge party in my honor at the hippest club in New York City. Everybody who is *anybody* is invited.

HERE'S HOW IT IS:

My eyes pop open on Sunday morning. I have officially entered teendom.

I take a deep breath and hold it, waiting to feel . . . changed. I wait for as long as I possibly can.

Exhale.

I don't feel any different at all.

But still I wait.

I wait for Dad to burst into my room, singing "HAPPY BIRTHDAY TO YOU!" at the top of his lungs, like always.

I wait for Mom to dive onto my bed and smother me with kisses, like always.

And then I remember.

Nothing about this summer is anything like always.

I am in mourning for my life.

For real.

I push myself out of bed and head down the hall. Dad's room is empty, as usual. And so is the kitchen and the rest of the house.

Today happens to be a Free Sunday, and I have a sinking suspicion that Dad has totally forgotten it's also my birthday. But then another thought pops into my head: What if Dad is choosing to forget in order to punish me for being such a coward?

"Why didn't you remind me it was your birthday?" Stella appears then, still in her pajamas. She gives me an annoyed look, as if the fact that *she* forgot my birthday is *my* fault. "Mom just called me on my cell. I didn't even, like, get you anything."

"'I am in mourning for my life,'" I mumble.

"Oh, stop saying that!" She puts her hands over her ears. "I'm sick to death of that line."

"It's a really cool line!"

"Well, I wish I could give it to you."

"Me too."

After Stella has fixed herself some tea, she uncharacteristically invites me into her room.

"Hey, you wanna pick something from my no-no cabinet since I don't have a present for you? Something special?"

"Sure." I act like it's no big deal, but it is.

Stella's no-no cabinet holds her most precious items. Things she's been collecting since she was a little girl, like china animals and glass ballerinas and little teacups and candles shaped like animals and playbills from plays she's seen and souvenirs from trips we've taken. The no-no cabinet has always been strictly hands-off, but today she unlocks the glass door and lets me choose what I want—with limits.

"No Tina" (her favorite glass ballerina). "And no Ba-ba" (an ancient china lamb).

I take my time deciding and finally choose a small ceramic apple with the words "New York City— Take a bite!" written in glittery lettering across it. Something she bought on a trip with Dad a couple of years ago.

"So predictable." Stella rolls her eyes, but she seems relieved that I didn't choose something older, more precious. And she doesn't kick me out of her room immediately, like she usually does. We sit on her bed while she brushes out her long golden locks and I roll the apple around in my hands, watching the glitter.

"You know," Stella begins, "it wasn't your fault . . . about Trace. I didn't know either. About the Asp— whatever it's called. Dad never told me. I guess he forgot. He's so preoccupied lately." A pregnant pause. "I just thought Trace was kind of . . . oh, I don't know . . . kind of weird too."

I glance into Stella's face, surprised. I can't believe she's actually trying to make me feel better, that she's actually being nice without someone (like Simon) telling her to.

"It doesn't matter. I shouldn't have said that." I look back down at the apple. "And I still have to apologize."

"You haven't said you're sorry yet?"

I shake my head.

"Well, it's not easy. Saying you're sorry." Stella's voice is strangely quiet, and I'm not totally sure, but all at once I have this feeling that she's not just talking about Thespis, that maybe she's actually talking about herself. Maybe she's even trying to apologize to *me*, for not playing the Nice Sister for so long.

"It's not easy." I glance up at her and we both kind of smile.

Now there's a weird, awkward moment. We're so used to bickering, I'm not sure what to say next.

"Well, you'll have a chance to say you're sorry today." Stella breaks the silence.

"What do you mean?"

"I think Mom invited Trace to your party."

My stomach does a little flip-flop. Why would Mom have invited Thespis without even asking me?

"Do you think Simon told Mom about what I said?" I ask, biting my lip.

"I don't think so." Stella shakes her head. "I think Simon would want you to tell her." Stella gets up and starts looking through her drawers, pulling out clothes, holding them up in front of the mirror. "She invited Scott, too, and Simon and a bunch of other people."

"Dad?" It just pops out, and then for some reason, I feel suddenly hopeful.

"I don't think so, Junebug." Stella gives me a quick glance.

A bubble of a moment. I can feel it hovering over us. Now is the time to ask Stella why everything is different this summer.

"What's going on with Dad?" I ask, kind of breathless.

Stella does another quick glance. "You mean the midlife crisis?" The tone is definitely dry.

Midlife crisis.

I've heard those words before. In movies. On TV. But I don't really know what they mean. So I just keep staring at Stella, waiting for her to explain.

"You know." She shrugs. "How men get to a certain age and they want to feel young again?"

Now it's like Stella is quoting something she's heard before, something from a talk show, probably. She watches a lot of TV.

I still don't get it, though. "What do you mean?"

Stella rolls her eyes. "Oh, Junebug, you're too young to understand."

"I'm thirteen!" I cry out. "I'm not a baby!"

"Oh, wow, thirteen!" Stella makes a face, and I start

to get up to leave, but then she says, "Sorry, Junebug. It's just . . . I guess when men get old—"

"Dad's not old," I interrupt.

"When they get *middle-aged*," Stella starts again, "sometimes they get tired of the way things are. They want things to be, I don't know, the way they used to be."

"Mom's the one who left," I say in a quiet voice, holding the apple tight in the palm of one hand.

"Yeah, but Dad's been kind of nutty lately. I mean, he never takes Mom's advice about what kind of plays to do, he never listens to her."

I open my mouth to speak, but Stella cuts me off.

"Look, I know you're Dad's little Mini-Me and you like tragedy and all that," she says. "But a lot of the plays are boring with a capital *B*. And, like, the Blue Moon is losing money because people just don't want to come to see boring plays."

I don't know what to say. I've never thought about money, even though I know we never have enough. Things are always tight, especially in the summer.

"Real Theater is important," I whisper finally. "Dad's always said that. It's nothing new. It's not a midlife crisis or whatever."

"Yeah, but Dad's just kind of crazed this summer. He's put himself in all the leads. He's never done that before. And he's even more of a Roadrunner than usual, like he's *afraid* of slowing down." Stella glances sideways, like she's not sure she should keep going. "And he's totally gaga over Lelia, which is really gross if you ask me because she's, like, half his age."

There. It's all out in the open. It's all stuff I've noticed myself and haven't wanted to put into words. But for some reason, hearing it from Stella makes the anger bubble up, like hot lava.

"It's not true!" I splutter. "We're short on men this year, that's why he's put himself in the plays, and Mom is the one who left, and he's not gaga over Lelia."

Stella is looking at me like I'm an idiot, like I'm a little kid who just doesn't get it.

And maybe I am a little kid.

Oh, wow, thirteen!

Big deal.

Maybe I'm still a baby after all.

"What's going to happen at the end of the summer?" I ask in a baby voice. "Will Mom and Dad get a divorce?"

"I don't know." Stella sighs. "I really don't, Junebug."

No *bug*. And what's more, Stella actually comes over and hugs me. It's a quick hug—and a little awkward since I can't remember the last time she actually hugged me—but it doesn't matter. It's a hug.

"Hey, you better hurry up and change out of your pajamas and brush your hair while you're at it," Stella says, abruptly turning back to the mirror. "You don't want to look like a total slob at your own party."

Wordlessly I head back to my own room and pick the black dress Simon made. It's like my second skin now. And then I brush out my hair and pull it back into a ponytail.

When we get to the farmhouse, Mama Duvall hugs all the breath out of me and then she orders me into the living room to greet my guests. (MAMA DUVALL, *Southern grandma, big and round, opinionated, orders people around kind of like a general*.)

In the living room, Mimi is the first to see me. "Happy birthday, my dear, sweet girl," she cries, and gives me two quick kisses, one on each cheek.

Scott comes and puts an arm around my shoulders

and gives a friendly squeeze. "Hey, birthday girl, happy birthday!"

"Um, thanks," I manage to mumble, nearly falling to the floor. I can't believe Scott actually *squeezed* me.

Simon is next. A kiss for my forehead. "Happy birthday, *dahling*," he murmurs.

Tears! Right on cue.

Immediately I turn away so Simon won't see them.

I've avoided Simon all week. It's been forever since I've heard *dahling* spoken to me, and I'm so glad to hear it now, and yet there's a part of me that wonders if the *dahling* is as *dahling* as it used to be.

Now I wait for Mom to give me a big hug, but she is sitting on the couch, talking to someone. Two someones.

Thespis and his mom.

"That's really interesting," my own mom is saying. "Junebug tells me you know so many interesting things about the theater."

"Oh, Trace just knows everything there is to know!" Mrs. Weaver cries in her deep Southern twang. She looks up then and waves. "Ah, there's the birthday girl!"

Mom jumps up and gives me a hug. Instead of melting into her arms like I thought I would, I just stand stiff as a board and let her hug me. I can feel Thespis and his mom watching from the couch. I wonder if Thespis's mom only came here to tell me what a terrible person I've been to her son.

Mom takes a step back to peer at me, a puzzled look on her face. I can tell she knows something's wrong, but I can't tell her what it is right now. She gives me a kiss and another quick hug and moves on to Stella.

"I've missed you so much!" she cries. "Tell me about being Miranda! And now you're Masha! And what are you next?"

"Just a member of the chorus." Stella rolls her eyes. "Bor*ing*!"

I want to scream. Stella is so lucky and she doesn't even know it. She's had tons of lines already this summer and with CHORUS, she has even more.

"D-d-did you know that in Greek plays the ch-ch-chorus is always a group of men or women who go around t-talking about the p-people in the p-play?" Thespis asks no one in particular. He's gazing down at his shoes, his hair falling over his eyes.

"Kind of like the old busybodies on our street, huh?" Mrs. Weaver says loudly, nudging her son, and everybody laughs.

Mama Duvall calls us loudly to dinner and everyone jostles toward the dining room. I feel a hand on my arm, stopping me.

It's Mrs. Weaver, of course. I take a breath and wait. I know she's going to let me have it.

"I just want to thank you for being so helpful to Trace."

I feel my cheeks burning. I can't look her in the eye. Is she being sarcastic?

"At home he talks about nothing but the Blue Moon and the actors and your daddy. And you."

I'm waiting for the thunder and lightning, and the anger. But nothing like that happens. In fact, she's smiling—beaming. And there are tears in her eyes.

"He has a really hard time connecting, you know. With people. He's been talking about the theater stuff for so long now. And I hardly pay any attention to it. I don't understand half of what he says! He never talks about school or other kids. He's never fit in anywhere before. But now he does. And it's just been so . . . great for him."

In a rush, Thespis's mom seizes me up in her grizzly bear of a hug. And just like Thespis did on that first day at the Blue Moon, I stand perfectly still.

I know I don't deserve this woman's hug. I don't deserve her gratitude. Not at all.

"I'm sorry," I whisper, but it's too faint to be heard.

Thespis is standing behind his mother. I can't see over her shoulder whether he's actually looking at me or not.

"I'm sorry," I whisper a little louder this time, but it's lost in Mama Duvall's booming voice.

"We're all waiting for you, birthday girl!"

"Here she comes!" Thespis's mom calls back, laughing. She releases me, wiping at the corners of her eyes.

The dining room table is full of people and food. Everybody eats, talking and laughing at once, complimenting Mama Duvall on her cooking. The dishes are all my favorites, but I hardly even taste what's on my plate.

The knot is there, in my stomach, tight as a fist.

I keep glancing from one face to another, finally to Thespis's face, across the table. He's picking at his food too.

And then it's cake time, and everybody sings.

"Happy birthday to you! Happy birthday to you!"

I'm smiling, I know I am, but it feels like I'm wearing a mask.

Is it a good-guy mask or a villain mask?

I don't know anymore. I definitely *feel* like a villain. I feel like DEATH, *hateful to mankind, loathed by the gods.*

After cake, it's gift time, which makes everything worse. How can I sit and smile and accept gifts when I'm so very flawed, when I'm such a terrible coward?

Mom's gift is first: a box of black T-shirts and tank tops and a gauzy black peasant skirt that she made herself.

"'Cause a little bird told me it's somebody's favorite color this summer!" Mom singsongs.

"'I am in mourning for my life!'" Stella places the back of her hand across her brow, all melodrama. I can tell she's mimicking me mimicking her.

Everybody laughs.

"Really, Junebug should be Masha," Stella says. "Black suits her, that's for sure."

Mom turns to me. "Oh, say the line," she says, laughing. "Do Masha. I want to see."

Everybody is staring at me now, waiting.

Any other time I would have loved the chance to perform in front of a crowd. I would have acted out MASHA's entire scene.

Any other time but this very moment.

I open my mouth to speak. I want to apologize to Thespis at last. I know I must or I'm simply going to burst. All the hatefulness spewing out of me.

But then something shifts.

"Maybe you should come see the show for yourself."

I know I'm the one who said the words, but I don't recognize my own voice. It's sharp as a knife.

Now there's complete silence. My audience is riveted, a roomful of eyes focused on me, just like I've always dreamed of.

"Well . . . you're . . . right, Junebug," Mom stammers, her eyes blinking in surprise. "I should come see a play . . . but, well . . . I guess I've been so busy. . . ."

"Too busy to come home?"

"Your father and I . . . you know we decided to . . . take a break for the summer."

"What does that mean? Take a break?"

My hands are shaking. In fact, I'm shaking all over. And my heart is thumping so hard and so loud, I'm sure everyone in the world can hear it.

"Does it mean you're getting a divorce?"

There. The words are out. In the open.

I look up at Mom, and her face seems to crumble, like a little girl about to cry. I want to take the question back, but at the same time, I want an answer. I want it now.

"June, honey, this really isn't a good time to talk about it." Mom's voice is so, so sad. It should break my heart, but it doesn't. My heart is hard as stone. I'm not just wearing the villain mask, I'm a villain through and through.

"Why not? When is a good time? You live here now and Dad lives at home, but he's never there."

"June—"

"And why did you name me June, anyway? It's a dumb name. I wasn't born in June! Beck and Stella got the good names—names that mean something. I'm just Junebug. An insect. A beetle."

"Well . . . honey . . . it's when we thought you were coming, and we didn't have time to pick another name, we were just so busy—"

"Busy, busy, busy! You're always so busy. . . ." My voice starts to crack, but I won't let it. "Dad was so busy he couldn't even bother to remember my birthday."

I stand up then and push past Mom, rushing for the door. The tall grass whips at my legs as I run through the fields. The cows turn to stare at me and then startle away.

They should be frightened! I am fearsome. I am *hateful to mankind, loathed by the gods.* I feel it pulsing through every bit of me.

The house is empty as usual. No sign of Dad. Of course.

Inside my room I slam the door behind me. I shut my eyes and breathe deeply. From the very center of my soul. Something Dad has always told me to do to calm my nerves.

And maybe it does help. Onstage. But not now. Not in real life.

I open my eyes and fling myself onto the bed,

falling on top of a small package wrapped in plain brown paper. I sit up and rip the paper. Inside is a book.

An Actor's Handbook by Constantin Stanislavski.

Dad's copy. I recognize it from his bookshelves. Inside, on the first page, there's a handwritten note:

For my dearest June Olivia—

A gift for you on the occasion of your thirteenth birthday—nearly overlooked, I fear. I hope you can forgive my forgetfulness, and that you will cherish this book as I have. Onstage and off, I have always found wisdom in these pages.

I love you with all my heart and soul—

Your father,

Cassius Harlan Cantrell

The book is small. It fits perfectly inside my hands. On the back cover, the blurb explains how Stanislavski is the "Father of Method Acting."

I know Dad used to be a "Method Actor" in New York. During a performance he would stay in character the whole time—during breaks, during intermission. Other actors would have to address him in character backstage or he wouldn't respond at all.

Dad's not really into the Method anymore. He still really gets into his character, but he doesn't go so deep.

"Too much to worry about now," he'll say. "Too much interference with the process."

I think "interference" must mean all the stuff he has to do besides acting to make sure the Blue Moon is running smoothly.

Now I open the book and start flipping through the pages. It's like a dictionary of all Stanislavski's teachings, everything in alphabetical order. I go to the end and open it to a page at random.

Under "Walking on the Stage," I read:

```
Let us learn to walk all over again
from the beginning, both on the stage
and off.
```

It sounds funny, and yet that's exactly what it feels like this summer. Like I'm learning to walk again. Like I'm a baby. I don't feel thirteen at all.

I flip to another page. Under "Role Inside the Actor," I find:

> The actor ceases to act, he begins to live
> the life of the play. . . . The author's
> words become his words. . . . This is
> a . . . *miracle* . . . for the sake of which
> we are willing to make any sacrifices, to
> be patient, suffer and work.

I close the book and hold it to my heart. The words are so beautiful. They describe exactly what I want to do at this moment—cease to exist. I want Junebug, the villain, to go away. I want Junebug, the good guy, the hero of the story, to return. I want to be like a true actor, living the life of a play, *becoming* something—someone—else.

Once more I open the book, and under "Actor as a True Artist," a line jumps out at me:

An actor has to have more than his
artistic talents, he must be an ideal
human being.

I read the words out loud once, twice. I stare at the page, and the letters start to blur.

An ideal human being.

The tears are falling—*plop*—raindrops on the page.

I wasn't an ideal human being today. In fact, I haven't been much of an ideal human being all summer.

I'm about to curl up into a ball on the bed and let myself bawl like a baby, when another thought hits me.

I haven't been an ideal human being, but neither has Dad.

The tears dry up—*poof*—just like that. The hatefulness starts bubbling up again. My heart is pounding fast, faster.

I replay everything that's happened this summer, a kaleidoscope of quick scenes, flashbacks in a movie.

The pounding is getting louder inside my ears. I am a storm—with thunder and lightning. I can feel the electricity, the spark.

I wish I had a sheet of tin of my very own inside

my room. I would pound my fists against it. I would make sure that everybody for miles around could hear me. And I wouldn't stop just because it said I should in the script. I would write my own script, my own play. I would roll thunder until all the thunder was rolled out of me.

V.

HERE'S HOW I SEE IT:

I go find Dad and tell him everything I hate about this summer.

I hate that Mom left, and that Dad let her leave.

I hate that I'm the one who had to choose for the summer between Mom and Dad. I hate that I had to take sides.

I hate that Dad is gaga over another woman, when the only woman he should be gaga over is his own wife (my mom!).

I hate that the woman Dad is gaga over is Lelia, who seems nice, but maybe isn't, who seems like she likes Dad, but maybe doesn't because maybe all she wants to do is wrap Dad around her little finger.

I hate how Dad brought Thespis here without even telling me anything about him, like the fact that he wasn't meant to be an understudy, a replacement.

And finally, I hate that Dad never talks to me anymore, never really tells me anything important, so that I've ended up feeling like I feel the rest of the lonely year when the Blue Moon is closed: invisible.

HERE'S HOW IT IS:

I'm still a coward.

I can't imagine actually going to Dad and telling him face-to-face what I hate about the summer, what I hate about him.

Maybe if I had a script to follow, maybe if it was all written out, I could say the lines without messing them up, without getting confused.

And that's when it hits me.

A script.

That's what I'll do. I'll write it all down. And then I'll give him the lines to read, just like a play.

Quickly, before anybody comes to stop me (like Mom or Stella or Dad himself more), I rummage through my desk drawers and find a notebook and a pen. I sit at my desk and start writing.

By the time I'm finished, my hand is cramping. And the writing is wild. I've underlined words and jammed in exclamation points. I've filled five whole pages with my hatefulness.

And the thing is, I feel a whole lot better.

I feel empty, light as air.

I sit staring down at the pages I've written. And then carefully I tear them out of the notebook and fold them up like a letter. I rummage through the drawers again and find an envelope and the wax kit my mom gave me for my birthday last year. It has my initials, *JOC*, in fancy blood red letters.

I put the pages in the envelope and then I seal the envelope closed.

Now the letter looks official. And dramatic. Exactly like a Prop in a play.

I head down the hallway and place the letter right on Dad's pillow.

And then I go back to my room, to my bed. I open *An Actor's Handbook* again, flip through the pages, but I can't seem to focus on the words this time. I keep listening for sounds of my dad—or Stella—coming home, but an hour passes and then another. My lids begin to feel heavy. I close my eyes, and everything fades to black. Just like that.

VI.

HERE'S HOW I SEE IT:

The whole summer was a bad dream. When I open my eyes I realize that everything is just the way it used to be.

Mom and Dad still live in the same house. My family is still a family. I am not like DEATH, *hateful to mankind, loathed by the gods.*

I am not a villain.

HERE'S HOW IT IS:

My eyes pop open. The light streaming through my window doesn't look like late afternoon sunlight.

I turn to the clock on my nightstand.

The bright red numbers say 11:05. I squint to make sure that what I'm seeing really is a.m., not p.m.

Eleven a.m.!

That means I must have slept through Sunday afternoon and Sunday night and all the way into Monday morning!

O Zeus!

I don't think I've ever slept so long in my whole entire life.

I sit up in bed, and then it hits me. If it's Monday, rehearsal for *Alcestis* was supposed to start at nine thirty sharp. *From the top!* as Dad always says.

Now I jump to my feet. I'm still wearing Simon's black dress from yesterday. I take a quick glance at myself in the mirror. The dress is okay, not too wrinkled. I run a brush through my hair and then I start down the hall.

And that's when I hear coughing.

Dad's coughing.

I freeze.

And that's when it all comes back to me.

A storm, with thunder and lightning. A flurry of writing. A letter left on a pillow like a Prop in a play.

My heart starts pounding. Not thunder anymore. Just my heart.

What if Dad's already read the note? What if he's

waiting to talk to me? Why else would he be home when he should be at the Blue Moon, in rehearsal?

Slowly I begin a silent retreat, backward, to my own room. But a voice stops me.

"Junebug, is that you? Are you there?"

Dad's voice sounds strange, kind of slurred, like he's been sleeping too, which is totally unlike him.

Plenty of time to rest in the grave!

"Junie?" Dad calls again.

"It's me—" My voice cracks. I clear it and try again. "It's me. I'm here."

"Junebug—"

I take a deep breath, from the very center of my soul, and force myself to walk down the hall. One foot in front of the other. Silently I stand in the doorway.

Dad is lying flat on his bed. It's like he's wearing makeup, which is weird because why would he be wearing makeup this early? His face is kind of a grayish color and the circles under his eyes are even darker than usual. He lifts his head off the pillow a bit and smiles, but it's more like a grimace.

"I was feeling . . . a little tired, and I came up to rest

for a few minutes and—" He lies back down and waves a hand in the air.

My eyes dart around for the letter, but I don't spot it anywhere—in his hands, on the floor, on the bed beside him. Dad must have read it. And it made him sick. He definitely looks sick.

"Junebug—I think—" He grimaces again.

"Dad, I'm sorry!" I rush toward him. "I'm sorry!"

Dad takes my hand and holds it tight.

"Listen, Junebug." His voice is just a whisper now. "It's okay. Everything is going to be okay. But listen to me. I need you to pick up the phone and dial 911. Now."

after

I.

HERE'S HOW I SEE IT:

Everything is going to be okay, just like Dad said.

HERE'S HOW IT IS:

Nothing is ever going to be okay again.

I gave my dad a heart attack.

"Junebug, tell me what happened!"

Mom takes me by the shoulders and peers into my face. Beck and Mama Duvall are standing behind her.

I gave my dad a heart attack.

I'm about to say it, but I don't have to. A nurse appears out of nowhere to confirm everything.

"Mrs. Cantrell, it appears your husband has suffered a heart attack."

"Where is he? Can I see him?" Mom whirls this way and that—an actor without any direction.

"The doctors are with him now, and they'll be able to speak with you soon, but there are some forms to fill out. Could you come with me, please?"

Mom nods. She pulls me to her in a swift hug, and then she's gone.

Mama Duvall and Beck lead me to a padded bench. Mama Duvall orders me to sit down and then she sits with me and puts an arm around me.

"Tell me what happened, Junebug," she commands, a general like usual, but it's okay. I want somebody to tell me what to do, what to say.

I gave my dad a heart attack.

The words won't come and so I try other words.

"He was . . . lying on . . . his bed." My teeth are chattering so hard I can hardly speak. I can't stop shivering. "He looked sick . . . his face was gray . . . he told me to call 911."

Mama Duvall takes off the long-sleeved blouse she's

wearing over a T-shirt and wraps it around me. She holds me in her arms and rocks me like a little baby. Now she doesn't feel like a general at all.

I keep waiting for Mom to come back, but she doesn't, and then Stella arrives with Scott. She bursts into tears when Beck tells her what happened.

Simon makes his entrance and immediately comes to sit on the other side of me and says "good girl" when Mama Duvall gets to the part about me calling 911.

"My brave *dahling*," he murmurs into my hair, hugging me close.

I gave my dad a heart attack.

I melt into his arms, even though I know I'm not a good girl or a *dahling*.

I gave my dad a heart attack.

Slowly the entire Blue Moon company begins to trickle into the waiting room. George and Coleman and Mimi and the other actors and apprentices. Everybody. Even Lelia.

And then Mom appears and we all gather in close.

"The doctors said that Cass had a heart attack— a pretty big one. And they're not sure—" Her voice breaks off. "They need to keep monitoring him in case there's another."

Now everybody's talking at once—sympathy, surprise, disbelief.

"That's the bad news—that he may have another." Mom takes a deep breath. "The good news is: He got here so quickly." She turns to me. "If Junebug hadn't been there with Cass and called the ambulance right away, well . . ." She doesn't finish the sentence.

Now everyone is looking at me. I want to change masks. I want everyone to know for sure. I'm not the hero. I'm really the villain. I was there to help Dad, but not before I hurt him.

II.

Here's how I see it:

The Blue Moon is never, ever dark.

The show must go on!

Here's how it is:

SHOW CANCELLED UNTIL FURTHER NOTICE

That's what the sign says. George painted it himself and hung it across the usual Blue Moon sign.

I have to pass it every time I go back and forth to the hospital.

And that's all I do for the next few days.

Back and forth.

Back and forth.

The first time I go back home I search Dad's room. Under the pillow, behind the bed, beneath the covers, but I can't find the letter.

Maybe Dad was so upset he burned the letter. (That happened in a play we did once. The actor had to burn a note right after he read it in an ashtray onstage.)

No sign of matches or ash though.

Maybe Dad was so distraught he tore the pages into tiny bits.

No sign of paper pieces in any of the garbage cans.

Back and forth.

Back and forth.

The first time they let me into intensive care to see Dad, I can't believe my eyes. The man lying in the hospital bed with all the tubes coming out of his arms and his nose doesn't look anything like PROSPERO or TRIGORIN or ADMETUS.

He doesn't look anything like my own beloved Daddy-o.

The man lying in the hospital bed looks small and old. And breakable.

And it's all my fault.

"I'm sorry."

I whisper the words. I'm too afraid to actually reach out and touch him. Afraid I'll hurt him even more.

Dad's eyes flutter open. His fingers find mine along the metal bed rail, and he gives a half squeeze. And that's all.

What does a half squeeze mean? That he forgives me?

His eyes close again.

Plenty of time to rest in the grave.

A shudder runs through me.

"Don't sleep, Daddy-o! Please. Don't sleep!" I cry out.

"Oh, honey, it's the medication," Mom says, putting an arm around me. "He'll be stronger soon, you'll see."

Mom can sew, but she can't act. I can tell she's faking it. She's not sure he'll get stronger. I can hear it in her voice and when I gaze at her face I can see it in her eyes.

"Mom?"

I want to tell her everything. The weight of what I've done is so heavy. Concrete blocks holding me down. I can barely move. I can barely breathe.

"Yes, Junebug?"

"I'm sorry! I'm sorry about what I said at my birthday, I'm sorry. . . ." The words come out in a rush.

Mom shakes her head. She turns and takes me in her arms.

"No, no, *I'm* the one who's sorry," she whispers. "Your father and I . . . we should have talked to you. We should have explained. Sometimes things happen and two people . . . two married people . . . they grow apart, and it's nobody's fault. It's not your fault, Junebug. It's nobody's fault. . . ." Her voice trails off. She's rocking me gently, back and forth. "You know, I was already calling you Junebug before you were born. Inside my belly. Your father wanted to name you something else, especially when you were born in July."

I've never heard this before. "What did he want to name me?" I ask.

"Imogen," she says. "From one of his favorite Shakespeare plays. I can't remember which one."

"Imogen," I repeat, and something clicks. It's the name of the daughter from *Cymbeline*! The play I chose out of the blue, out of embarrassment, the Shakespeare play I've never read.

"But I wanted to stick with June—with Junebug— because . . . well, I guess because I felt like Cass had chosen the names before, and they were theater names. But I wanted to choose this time. A name of my own. And you were already my little Junebug."

I let all this sink in. I look up at Mom.

"It's okay," I whisper. "I don't mind. I know I'm not a beetle. And I don't think I'm an Imogen either."

Mom smiles through her tears. "Neither do I."

Dad makes a coughing sound, and instantly we both turn toward him. His eyes flutter open for a moment and close again. The coughing stops. His chest continues to rise and fall, the pattern of his heartbeat zigzagging in green on a monitor above his head.

I glance from the monitor to Mom's face. She's

watching Dad. She reaches out and tenderly caresses his cheek.

She still loves him. I'm sure of it. She can sew but she can't act. I can see the love right there, in her face, in her eyes.

"Would you die for Dad?" I ask suddenly. The question from *Alcestis*.

Mom turns to me again, her brow wrinkling.

"Would you give your life so another might live?" I say it the way Dad said it in rehearsal.

Now Mom gets it, but she waves a hand in the air, dismissing the question.

"Oh, Junebug, you only have choices like that in plays, not in real life," she says in a tired voice.

"But if you did have the choice. If you knew for certain Dad was going to die, and the only way to save him was to give your own life. Would you do it? Would you take his place?"

Mom turns back to Dad. She leans over to smooth a lock of hair from his forehead. She doesn't say anything for a long time, so I think she's going to simply ignore the question. But then she says, quietly, so I almost miss it:

"Yes, I would."

III.

HERE'S HOW I SEE IT:

I step out onto the stage and say the words I was destined to say.

"'I am in mourning for my life.'"

HERE'S HOW IT IS:

I do step out onto the stage, but I can't say the words. I won't. I don't want to be in mourning for my life. Not anymore.

The Blue Moon stage is empty, silent. The cast and crew are all scattered, some of them holed up in their rooms, some at the hospital. Everyone is waiting, waiting to see what will happen to Dad, to the rest of the Blue Moon season.

Center stage I stand and slip the beastie over my head. I close my eyes and breathe in the familiar scent.

Makeup and sweat.

I was practically weaned on the stuff. And that's why even just a whiff makes life bearable. For the moment.

I am still so heavy with my secret—so very heavy.

And now I am wearing the mask of a beast. And so I whisper one of CALIBAN'S lines, the words echoing around inside the beastie head.

"And then, in dreaming, the clouds methought would open and show riches ready to drop upon me that, when I waked, I cried to dream again."

That's exactly what I want.

I want my life to be how I see it, not how it is.

I want Mom to come home.

I want us all to run the Blue Moon together, a family again.

And above all things I want Dad to get well. I want his heart to be whole.

I turn and make my exit. Backstage is empty too. The Men's Dressing Room is silent as a tomb. But Dad's giant black toolbox is still where he left it.

Tools of the actor's trade.

I sit in Dad's chair and remove the beastie head. Slowly I open the lid.

Tins of foundation. Tubes of rouge. Brown and black pencils to line the face, to make Dad look older or more fierce or just plain different. Fake eyebrows and furry beards and a big fake rubbery nose.

I run my fingers lightly over everything. I pick up the powder brush—one of the things Dad would have touched last—and grasp the handle. I brush the soft bristles over my face, dusting myself with leftover powder.

"D-d-did you know that in the old d-days stage makeup was called greasepaint and it was made out of lead, so actors b-back then often didn't live very long because they got lead poisoning?"

Enter Thespis.

I start to reach for the beastie. My face is so puffy and swollen and red from crying over the last few days that I don't want to be seen. But Thespis isn't looking at my face, as usual, so it doesn't matter.

"Dying for your art," I mumble. "How noble."

Thespis chuckles. At least I think it's a chuckle. It's in between a cough and a snort. I realize I've never actually heard him laugh before.

"How's your d-dad?" Thespis asks now.

"The same."

"M-m-mom said if there's anything we c-can do . . ."

I nod. It's what everybody offers.

And O how I wish there was something somebody could do.

O how I wish I could be like PROSPERO and wave a magic wand in the air and make Dad's illness vanish—*poof!*—just like that.

O how I wish I could be like Dad when he's Director and clap my hands together and everything would start over, from the top so I wouldn't have left the letter on Dad's pillow.

"I gave my dad a heart attack."

The words aren't inside my own head anymore. They're out in the open!

It's such a shock, I start giggling. I put a hand over my mouth to stop the laughter. And then I'm shivering, just like I did at the hospital that first day. I'm not sure I'll be able to stop.

Thespis doesn't say a word, but he moves closer, sinking into the chair beside me.

I hold the powder brush tightly in my closed fists and I tell Thespis everything. I tell him about Mom leaving at the start of the summer. I tell him about Dad not talking to me like he used to. I tell him about Lelia and the gaga look Dad always gets around her. I tell him about what Christopher said and how I'm not sure if it's true or not.

And then I tell Thespis about the letter. I tell him everything I wrote, even the part about him.

It seems to take forever to get through it all, but when I'm finished talking, it's like the concrete blocks have been rolled away.

"See, if I hadn't given Dad the letter, he wouldn't have had a heart attack." I want to make sure Thespis understands because he hasn't said a word. "If I hadn't given Dad the letter he would be okay."

"That's not t-true," Thespis says at last. "Heart attacks happen because there's something wrong with the heart. The arteries are b-b-blocked or the valves aren't working p-properly or a portion of the heart is d-damaged."

His voice is completely matter-of-fact, like he's quoting from a science book.

I shake my head.

"It's my fault," I whisper. Maybe I shouldn't have told Thespis. How could he possibly get it?

"D-d-did you know," Thespis starts, and I'm about to cut him off because I don't want to hear any theater history right now, "that my dad d-d-died?"

I open my mouth to speak, but I can't.

My dad used to say I had a photographic memory.

Used to say.

Past tense.

I never even thought to ask Thespis about it. I never even thought to ask why he had a stepdad, or anything about his life outside the Blue Moon.

"When?" I ask now.

"F-f-four years ago."

"I'm sorry," I whisper.

"Right b-b-before my dad died, we had a f-fight. I wanted him to c-c-come to my school. It was father-son day. But Dad was too busy at work, and he said he c-couldn't. I got really mad b-because he was always too busy. He was always w-working. I told him that I hated him and that I didn't care if I never saw him again."

Thespis stops to take a breath. I know what's coming, but part of me doesn't want to hear it because I know it's going to be awful.

"When I g-g-got home from school that d-day, my aunts were there and Mom was crying. She told me there had b-been an accident—a c-c-c-car wreck.

That it happened really fast. Dad didn't feel any pain. The police said it was the other driver's fault, b-b-but I knew it wasn't. I knew it was my fault."

"But it wasn't your fault!" I cry out. "How could it possibly be your fault? You weren't in the car. You weren't even there."

"I know, b-b-but for a long time I thought it was my fault because of what I s-said. I told Dad I n-n-never wanted to s-see him again, and that's exactly what happened."

We're both silent. I don't know how long we sit there, side by side.

"That's terrible. I'm so, so sorry," I finally whisper. "But you have to know it wasn't your fault."

Thespis looks at me. Really looks at me.

"That's what I'm trying to tell you."

IV.

HERE'S HOW I SEE IT:

Everybody's theater.

That's what The Blue Moon Playhouse used to be.

And that's what it becomes once more.

HERE'S HOW IT IS:

"That makes three hundred and t-two," Thespis says as he hands out one of the last programs. "Exactly."

"Three hundred and two people," I whisper in awe.

"D-d-did you know that in the old d-days, a trumpet announced the opening of a p-play?"

"Cool. I wish we had a trumpet."

I gaze out at all the townies, all the bodies, filling every seat. In fact, we had to frantically bring other seats from anywhere we could find them—the dining area, the rehearsal hall, the actors' rooms. And even with extra chairs, bodies are overflowing onto the brick steps. But nobody seems to mind. Everybody is laughing, talking, eating, waiting for the show to begin.

"It's like the whole entire town has come out for Opening Night!" I whisper.

"I think they have, *dahling*."

Enter Simon. He puts an arm around my shoulders and together we take in the spectacle. It's just like he described—the first years of the theater. So many people! There are even kids from my school. Billy Cooper, for one. When I handed him a program and pointed out his seat, he said, "I'm really sorry about your dad," and he smiled at me and didn't seem like such a jerk anymore.

"They've all come out for Cass," Simon says. "Just like they did in the beginning."

"I wish Dad was here to see this."

Tears. Right on cue. So easy to do in real life.

"*Dahling*," Simon murmurs, holding me tighter against him. "You know he's here in spirit."

I nod, but I can't stop the gushing waterfall.

"And he'll be back—good as new—in no time. You'll see."

I keep nodding. I know Dad will be back, but it won't be exactly good as new.

The doctors found something wrong with his heart, something different from other hearts. They did a lot of tests and asked a lot of questions about family history—how so many Cantrells had died young of heart attacks.

So now I know for sure that Thespis was right. The heart attack wasn't my fault, exactly. But still I wish I hadn't given Dad the letter, because the doctors also talked about stress, how stress can make what's wrong with Dad's heart worse.

Now the doctors are going to operate to fix what's wrong, but first they have to wait. Dad has to rest and get stronger.

And so Dad is resting and getting stronger while we are keeping the Blue Moon going.

Simon and Mom took over and the whole company pulled together to keep the place running. Christopher learned ADMETUS's lines in no time flat. He'll play two roles, since DEATH wears a long cloak that covers him completely, and he's never in the same scene with ADMETUS.

The show must go on!

"We have exactly five minutes before Coleman calls places," Thespis announces, glancing down at his watch.

"*O Zeus!*" I cry out. "I've got to re-do my face!"

Simon holds me a moment longer and then releases me. "Break a leg, *dahling!*"

I rush backstage and fly into the Ladies' Dressing Room.

Lelia is there, the only one still putting the final touches on her face.

I've hardly spoken to Lelia since Dad had the heart

attack. Once rehearsals started up again, I was extra busy. I've only seen Lelia at the hospital twice, and that was always when I was leaving, so I don't know what her visits meant.

"Hey, Junebug," she says as I take my seat and begin to retouch my makeup.

"Hey," I answer back.

"You've done a really good job on your eyes." She glances at me in the mirror and gives the same bright smile as always.

"Thanks."

I close my eyes to dust my face with powder. When I open them, Lelia has come to stand behind my chair.

"I want you to have the book," she says, "the book about Sarah Bernhardt. I want you to keep it."

"Thanks." I'm not sure what else to say. "Are you sure?"

"Yeah, I'm sure." Lelia seems to hesitate. "You know, I get stage fright, just like Madame Sarah did. Maybe not so bad, because I'm not sure I need a coffin!"

She lets out a little laugh, and I allow myself to smile. I'd almost forgotten about the Prop Room coffin. I haven't wanted to go near it because even going near a coffin seems awful now. I haven't wanted to wear black either.

"I get really scared before I go onstage," Lelia continues. "But reading that book helped me see that even the greatest actresses get stage fright sometimes. Even the greatest actresses have doubts about who they are." She gazes at me in the mirror. "Do you ever get stage fright?"

I'm about to shake my head. I'm about to tell her that, no, I never get stage fright before a performance.

But then I think about how the Blue Moon will close in another few weeks, and how I don't know if it will ever open again. I don't know if Dad will be strong enough to do Real Theater anymore.

"Yeah, I do." I meet Lelia's eye in the mirror. "I get stage fright. Sometimes."

"Well, it'll just be our little secret, right?" She places her hand on my shoulder for a moment. And then she turns to leave. "Break a leg, Madame Junebug," she says, exiting the scene.

I look at myself in the mirror. "Break a leg."

V.

Here's how I see it:

I am an actress and this is my summer debut. The stage is silent, waiting. I step out from the wings and I am blind inside the light but I know the audience is out there, just beyond the glare. I can feel them. Hundreds of eyes, watching me.

I am breathing deeply, from the very center of my soul. I am waiting, waiting for the moment—not to speak any lines, for I am a *silent character*—but to simply *be* the person I'm meant to be.

I am getting ready to fly.

Here's how it is:

Silently, I follow Thespis across the stage.

Lelia is lying on a couch, the whole cast wrapped around her. Thespis kneels at her feet, and I do the same. I listen for our cue.

"'O wicked fortune!'" CHILD I/Thespis begins.

I take a deep breath and wait. Thespis has never actually made it through rehearsal without stuttering. I'm prepared to say his line if he gets completely stuck.

"'Mother has gone d-down there, Father, she is not here with us in the sunshine anymore,'" he continues.

O wonder!

Barely a stutter!

CHILD I/Thespis continues on, and only once does he fumble a word, but it seems totally natural, like he's truly in mourning, like he's so grief-stricken he can hardly speak.

And then the scene ends—*poof!*—just like that. And we're back in the wings, back in the dark.

"You did it!" I whisper to Thespis, grabbing onto his arms and pulling him toward the Prop Room so we won't be heard from the stage. "You got through the whole speech!"

"B-b-but we didn't cry," Thespis says, his brow wrinkling.

I stare at him a minute. I'd totally forgotten about crying because I was so worried about Thespis not stuttering.

"Tears, kids, we'll need tears by Opening Night!" I do a perfect imitation of Dad, and Thespis kind of snorts. This time I'm sure it's a laugh. So I laugh too.

"We'll cry tomorrow night," I tell him, "and the night after that, and the night after that." I watch his face. "We have enough stuff to use for our sad memory."

Thespis looks at me. Really looks at me. "Yeah, I guess we do."

And that's when it pops out.

"I'm sorry."

I take a deep breath. "I wasn't very nice to you this summer."

I wait. And wait.

Thespis is still looking at me.

"I know," he says finally, and then he shrugs and gives a little half smile. "But it's okay."

A pregnant pause, during which we both gaze at the floor.

"I guess we probably need to do some gofering, right?" I ask, breaking the silence.

"Right," Thespis answers, and together we head to the Green Room.

"How did you get into theater stuff anyway?" I ask, suddenly wanting to know more about Thespis. "I mean, it's not like your mom seems that into it."

"It was my d-d-dad. He liked doing plays in high school, but his f-family always made f-fun of him. So he stopped. But he'd always take me to Broadway shows when they'd come through town. And sometimes he'd act in the community theater where we lived."

I try to imagine how different things would be if Dad had acted out Grandpa Cantrell's version of his life.

"After Dad d-d-died, Mom d-didn't take me to plays," Thespis continues. "We couldn't afford it. And so I just started reading b-books. I never even thought about g-going onstage b-because . . . because I have trouble concentrating. B-because of my stutter."

I stop dead in my tracks and turn to stare at him.

"You mean, you've never gone onstage before this? Before tonight?"

Thespis shakes his head.

"But your mom said—"

"I know." The color is rising up from his collar all the way to his hairline. The pink flush of roses. "Mom k-kind of stretches the truth."

"You're kidding!"

Thespis shakes his head.

"Why didn't you tell me?" I cry, but then I answer my own question. "Why would you tell me? I wasn't very nice."

The guilt is there. Right on cue.

"I told your d-d-dad," Thespis says. "And he said that he'd read how theater could be g-good for people who stutter. That a lot of famous actors had some k-kind of speech impediment that they had to overcome. So your d-dad would work with me when he had time. Give me speech exercises."

I can't believe it! I was so jealous of Dad spending time with Thespis, and all Dad was doing was trying to help him.

"I d-d-didn't want the speaking p-part in *Alcestis*," Thespis continues. "I was scared. But your dad said it would be good for me."

"And he was right!" I cock my head at Thespis. "Courage. It's one of the most important things. If you want to be a real actor. That's what Dad always says." I pause, thinking it through. "And you have it. You have courage! I don't think I could have gone onstage, not knowing if I'd make it through a line or not. But you did it! And this was your big debut! How did it feel?"

"Not b-bad." Thespis studies the floor, his cheeks still pink. And then he grins. "Not bad."

After we've gofered some water and Mimi's usual drink, we sit in the Green Room, listening to the muffled sounds of the play.

"We'll be in the same grade when school starts up," Thespis says. "I go to regular school, you know."

"Alas, alack." I sigh. "I hate school."

"So d-do I. Kids always make fun of me."

My face goes straight to tomato—*poof*—just like that.

"They make fun of me, too," I tell him.

"I'm always the new k-kid," Thespis adds. "We've m-moved around a lot. I hate not knowing anybody."

There's a pause. But just a short one.

"Well, you know me."

We're not looking at each other, but something is changing. I can feel it.

"Did you know that I call you Thespis? In my head?" I blurt out. "It's because Dad said you were 'quite the young thespian' when you first got here, and it made me feel, I don't know, jealous."

Thespis's eyes slide sideways, to the wall, thinking it through.

"I like it," he says at last. "You c-can c-call me Thespis anytime you want."

I shake my head. "No, I think I should make you a real person. Not just a character."

"Okay," Thespis says with a shrug and another half smile.

And inside my head I'm rewriting the script.

TRACE WEAVER, *twelve years old; stutters a bit; kind of a strange fish, but really smart; knows a lot about theater history; has courage as well as a photographic memory; a friend.*

VI.

HERE'S HOW I SEE IT:

The Blue Moon is never ever dark. It remains open three hundred and sixty-five days a year.

The actors never leave.

The dorm rooms never become abandoned.

The Costume Room never gets filled with moth-balls and plastic coverings to keep the costumes safe for the winter.

The stage lights and sound equipment never get stored away.

The chairs never get stacked into rows in the rehearsal hall.

The stage never goes completely bare.

HERE'S HOW IT IS:

"Good-bye, good-bye!"

"Farewell!"

"Until we meet again!"

"Anon!"

The voices ring out. The players make their exits (all except Simon, who will stay on a while longer with us while Dad mends). The rooms empty out. The stage is bare.

Except for me.

I take my place center stage, and since Dad isn't here to do it himself, I utter one of PROSPERO/Dad's final summing up lines:

"'Our revels now are ended.
These our actors, as I foretold you,
Were all spirits,
And are melted
Into thin air, into thin air.'"

Hark?

I hear clapping, even though the house is empty.

Enter Stella, eyes all puffy, nose all red from blowing it so much.

She's been crying nonstop since Scott made his exit this morning, back to college. (They promised to e-mail and/or call every day.)

"I came to get you," she says between sniffles. "Dad's home."

"O Zeus!" I shriek. I can't believe I missed Dad's grand entrance! "I thought he wasn't supposed to get home till this afternoon!"

"They released him early, I guess."

I'm about to bound away, but Stella stops me.

"Junebug, wait. I've been meaning to give you this." She reaches into her back pocket and fishes out a folded-up square of paper.

It's my letter to Dad.

"Where did you get that?" I reach out and snatch it from her fingers.

"I found it when I was changing the sheets on Dad's bed."

"When did you change Dad's sheets?"

"Like, a few days after he went to the hospital."

"Where did you find it?"

"It was kind of stuck. In between the mattress and the frame."

I stare down at the letter in silence. How did I miss it when I searched everywhere?

"It was really wedged in there," Stella says, seeming to read my mind. And then she gives me a quick up and down. "Wow, you had a lot of pent-up anger in there, little sister!"

"Did you read it?" I cry out.

"Yeah, I couldn't help it." A shrug. "It was like a secret message or something."

"It *was* a secret message. For Dad's eyes only!"

"Well, he never read it."

"Huh?"

"It was still sealed when I found it."

All the air goes out of me. Like I've been punched in the stomach. And my knees go weak. I could just fall down on the stage right this very minute. A dead faint. Right on cue.

"He didn't read it," I whisper at last, staring down at the paper in my hands. "It wasn't my fault."

I know what Thespis said. I know what the doctors told us. But a part of me still felt like the heart attack was my fault. Dad wasn't supposed to have any stress. And the letter would definitely have caused him stress.

"You know, you could've come to me," Stella says. "I mean, you didn't have to keep all that stuff, like, bottled up inside." She reaches out and gently raps her knuckles against my forehead. "Earth to the bug brain." The words don't sound as harsh as they usually do. "You need to come out of there sometimes. Into the real world." She pauses to blow her nose. "Anyway, are you going to tell Dad all that stuff now? He's not supposed to get stressed out. And anyway, Lelia's gone."

"Yeah, I know." I wait a moment, and then I ask the question I've been scared to ask. "Is Mom coming back?"

"I don't know." Stella looks away. "I mean, Dad was kind of a jerk. He was definitely having a midlife crises, like I said."

"Mom still loves Dad," I announce. "Even if he was a jerk. She still loves him."

"How do you know?" Stella turns back to me.

"She said she'd give her life for him if she could."

Another gentle rap on the forehead.

"Hello in there. This is real life, not a play. In real life, people don't do things like that. In real life there's no script to follow."

"Well there should be," I say. "It would make things a lot easier."

Together we go back to the house. Mom's in the kitchen, fixing some lunch. I give her a great big hug and then she tells me that Dad has been asking for me.

I walk quietly down the hallway. At the door, I peek in without saying a word.

Dad is lying on his bed, propped up among the pillows. He doesn't look as small and old as he did in the hospital. He doesn't look so breakable.

Still I hesitate, afraid to do anything that might hurt him.

"How now, daughter?" Dad cries when he catches sight of me.

"How now, Daddy-o?" I reply in a tiny voice.

Dad watches me a moment, then says, "Not so bad I can't get a hug from my own Junebug!"

He opens his arms wide. I take a step forward, and then I'm on the bed, wrapped in a wonderful hug.

"My Junebug," Dad murmurs softly as I tuck my head under his chin. "Have you been saying your farewells?"

I nod, unable to speak.

"'Parting is such sweet sorrow,'" Dad quotes. I know the phrase, of course. Dad's said it often enough, but I don't know where it's from. "I've missed you," he says now, hugging me tighter.

"I've missed you!" I whisper back.

It feels so good to be wrapped tight in Dad's arms. Everything feels right again. I could stay like this forever.

"I'm sorry," Dad says, and I catch my breath, surprised, waiting to hear what his next line will be. "I'm sorry for a lot of things. But most of all I'm sorry for not being a very good father. I'm afraid I wasn't . . . quite myself . . . this summer."

His voice breaks. He clears his throat. "'One man in his time plays many parts . . .'" The quoting voice starts up, but then it stops. "I'm afraid . . . this summer . . . I played the fool."

And it's only Dad talking. Not Shakespeare. Not anybody else.

Just Dad.

"Definitely, I played the fool."

I don't move. I'm afraid to move, afraid to break the bubble. I don't think Dad has ever apologized to me. He's never had to. At least not before this summer.

"Forgive me, Junebug," he murmurs, his lips brushing the top of my head. "Forgive me. Please?"

Tears. Right on cue. So easy to do in real life. So easy.

And maybe I will use this memory later, one day, when I need to cry real tears onstage. But then again, maybe I won't.

"We wish your peace."

The words pop into my head and out of my

mouth. The words MIRANDA says to her own father, PROSPERO, when he seems sad. Dad lets out a short sound—a laugh or sob, I don't know which. He hugs me even tighter than before, and we stay that way a long, long time. And with my ear pressed flat against his chest I can hear his heart beating. It sounds strong, like always.

"Will the Blue Moon close for good?" I ask at last, afraid of what Dad will say, but needing to ask the question anyway.

A pregnant pause.

"Close?" Dad cries then. "Close the Blue Moon?!" He lets out a great sigh of mock exasperation and shifts me sideways so we are eye to eye. "Now, Junebug, haven't you learned anything at all, anything about theater?" His eyes are just like mine, big and green, and full of light and laughter. "What have I always, always told you? No matter what happens. No matter what catastrophes may befall you? What is the most important thing to remember?"

"The show must go on."

I chant the words I've heard my whole, entire life. Dad grins down at me and I grin back, and right

here's how i see it - here's how it is

on cue we take a deep breath and chant the words together.

"The show must go on!"

VII.

Here's how I see it/Here's how it is:

SCENE FROM OPENING NIGHT OF THE NEW BLUE MOON
PLAYHOUSE SEASON

> [Spotlight comes up on bedroom, Cantrell
> household. It is after midnight, after
> the family has returned from the Opening
> Night party. MOM and DAD are lying on
> the big cherry bed, their youngest
> daughter, JUNE, wedged between them.
> STELLA is perched on the edge of the
> bed—too old for cuddling, but still glad
> to be part of the scene. BECK is absent—
> working a job during his summer break
> from college. Excitedly the family talks
> about Opening Night—the full house, the

applause, the standing ovation, the thunderous laughter since the play was a real comedy for a change.]

DAD: Not bad for an Opening Night, eh, my ladies? [Glancing first at his wife, giving her a special smile, and then at his youngest daughter.] In fact, I might even say it was—
JUNEBUG: [Finishing the sentence.] Humming!
THE WHOLE FAMILY: [all together] Definitely humming!

The End

Acknowledgments

I would like to thank Caitlyn Dlouhy, wonderful friend and extraordinary editor, who never stopped believing in me and who guided this story through (at last!) to its final curtain; my husband, Tim Ungs, and our children, Daniel, Lila, and Theo, for their patience and love; my brother, Robby, for helping to keep the dream alive; and thank you to the Kentucky Arts Council, for giving me an Al Smith Fellowship exactly when I needed it most.

Author's Note

I grew up in a summer-stock theater much like the Blue Moon Playhouse, but not exactly like it. The characters in this book are "such stuff as dreams are made on," as PROSPERO says in *The Tempest*, but they were inspired by real life people, by an ever changing and fascinating ensemble cast in the play of my childhood.

Growing up in a theater was a magical experience. No other kid I knew had their very own costume room and prop room. No other kid I knew had parents who worked so hard to bring magic to life, night after night, summer after summer, year after year.

I did not become an actress, like I dreamed of when I was Junebug's age. I became a writer instead. Deep down I think I was always more of a listener, an observer, than a performer. And so I chose to write instead of act.

But my family's summer-stock theater is still alive

today, and going to a play is still one of my favorite things to do. There's nothing in the world quite like watching actors—live actors—performing a play right before your very eyes. There's nothing like sitting in the audience, waiting for the house lights to dim and the stage lights to come up, waiting for that moment, that magical moment, when an actor walks out upon the stage, and speaks the first line, and the play begins. . . .

The Plays From the Blue Moon Playhouse Season

The Tempest by William Shakespeare

PLOT: Sorcery, intrigue, revenge, and comedy are woven together in one of Shakespeare's most enchanting plays. A spell cast by PROSPERO, the exiled Duke of Milan, creates a mighty tempest that shipwrecks his betrayers and brings them to the barren island where he himself had been banished with his daughter MIRANDA a dozen years earlier. The spirit ARIEL reluctantly helps Prospero weave his spells, and the brutish, resentful slave CALIBAN is another unforgettable Shakespearean character.

BACKGROUND: *The Tempest* is believed to have been written by William Shakespeare around 1610 or 1611. It was performed only in adapted versions until the nineteenth century, when the Bard's own words were brought back into the text. It is now considered one of Shakespeare's greatest plays.

Sources: Shakespeare, William: *The Complete Works of William Shakespeare (Thirty-seven Volumes in One)*. New York: Walter J. Black, Inc., 1936.

absoluteshakespeare.com/index.htm

shakespeare-online.com

The Seagull by Anton Chekhov

PLOT: The setting is a summer home in the Russian countryside, and the action revolves around the conflicts, both romantic and artistic, that arise between an eccentric group of visiting friends and family, including a fading leading lady of the stage, Irina Arkadina; her new love interest, the famous writer Trigorin; and Arkadina's melancholy son who aspires to be a playwright.

BACKGROUND: *The Seagull* was written in 1895 and was a spectacular failure when it was first produced in 1896 in Saint Petersburg, Russia. The audience booed so loudly, the actors could barely be heard, and the playwright hid backstage for much of the performance.

In 1898 the play was revived by the Moscow Art Theatre, under the direction of Constantin Stanislavski, who had begun teaching a "method" of acting based on "real" emotion and action, rather than "pretend." This time, *The Seagull* was a huge success, and Chekhov went on to become one of the most celebrated and widely produced playwrights in Russia and throughout the world. Chekhov always maintained that *The Seagull* was a comedy, despite its sad ending.

Sources on Anton Chekhov, *The Seagull*, and the teachings of Constantin Stanislavski: Dunnigan, Ann, transl. *Chekhov, the Major Plays*. New York: Penguin Putnam, Inc., 1964.

Lahr, John. "Geography of Regret," *The New Yorker*, October 13, 2008, sec. "The Theatre."

Hapgood, Elizabeth Reynolds, ed. and transl. *An Actor's Handbook: An Alphabetical Arrangement of Concise Statements on Aspects of Acting*. New York: Theatre Arts, Inc., 1963.

————. *An Actor Prepares*. New York: Theatre Arts, Inc., 1963.

Alcestis by Euripides

PLOT: This is based on ancient legend about a king named Admetus, who has been condemned by the gods to die. Admetus, who was too cowardly to accept his fate, allows his devoted wife, Alcestis, to take his place. When Heracles, son of Zeus, arrives as an unexpected guest, Admetus pretends that he is not in mourning in order to be a good host. Heracles, in gratitude for his friend's selfless hospitality, travels to the underworld, battles Death, and brings Alcestis back to the land of the living.

BACKGROUND: *Alcestis* is believed to have been written and first produced around 438 BC in Athens, Greece. The playwright, Euripides, was not very popular in his own day, losing many coveted playwriting prizes to his contemporaries. But his acclaim grew after his death, and he is often referred to as the father of realism because he created characters with real feelings, like doubt and regret.

SOURCES: Grene, David, and Richard Lattimore, eds. *Euripedes I: Four Tragedies*. Chicago: University of Chicago Press, 1955.

Sources for information about theater history and about Madame Sarah Bernhardt: Billington, Michael. *The Guinness Book of Theatre Facts and Feats*. Enfield, Middlesex: Guinness Superlatives, 1982.

Skinner, Cornelia Otis. *Madame Sarah*. Boston: Houghton Mifflin, 1967.

**Turn the page for an excerpt
from *Dream of Night*,
Heather Henson's newest novel!**

Night

Brrr—

The sound comes sudden and sharp. Shrill. Like the call of a bird, but not. The sound is not a living sound—somehow he knows that—and it is everything.

rrrr—

The sound is flight, freedom.

nnnng—*!*

The sound makes his legs move. Before his brain even knows. He is moving. Exploding through the metal gate. Into space.

Not empty space. No. There are bodies in the way, blocking him. But he will move through the bodies just like he moved through the gate. Except he is being held up by the man on his back, and this makes him angry.

And so he fights. And fights. And fights.

To run.

To be faster than the rest.

To be leader of this pack.

To be the winner.

Tight inside the rush of bodies he smells rage and joy. He smells fear. He does not know which makes his legs move faster. All he knows is that he must run.

And so he does. He runs and runs and runs, and around the turn the man lets him go.

A little.

Bodies still in the way but now he can see the empty spaces between them. Because it's the empty spaces that matter in a race. An inch, a moment, a breath to slip through.

Open.

Close.

Open.

Close.

It's that quick. The space between the bodies. Too quick to think about. Time only to move.

And that's what he does.

Move.

One by one the bodies fall away. Until only two remain.

And still the man on his back won't let him go and still he keeps on fighting. It's all he knows how to do.

Fight and fight and fight. And run. As fast as he can possibly. Run. Just to be the best, the first, the winner of this race.

Nothing to hold him back now. Not even the man on his back. He is faster than the rest and he knows it and the man knows it and so the man lets him go at last.

Two bodies.

One.

Open space.

And that's when he hears it. That's when he always hears it. The sound that makes him run even faster.

A great roaring. Like the wind. Fierce and terrible. And beautiful, too. The most beautiful sound in the world.

Because the roaring means that he is winning, that he is flying.

Dream of Night is flying through air.

Eeeeee!

And then he isn't.

Eeeeee!

Something ripping him out of that time, long ago,

when he was a winner. Something pulling him back to where he is now.

Eeeeee!

The ground rumbles and shakes beneath his hooves. Light tears at the darkness. The roaring inside his head has disappeared.

Eeeeee!

He lifts his nose, inhales deeply. What he smells is fear and confusion. Panic.

What he smells is man.

"Hiya, hey! Hey! Hey!"

"Watch it! Whoa, whoa!"

Ears cupping the voices.

None belong to the man with the chains, but it doesn't matter. All men are the same. He hates every one.

"This sure's a wild bunch!"

"You said it."

"Get 'em to go this way."

Now he understands. Men have come to this place, strangers. And the mares are screaming, wild and frantic, to protect their young.

He lifts his head higher, calls out, but the mares can't hear. They are beyond hearing.

And so he stomps his hooves into the hard ground.

Pain like fire burns up his front legs, but he ignores it. He takes a great breath and rears back with every bit of strength he has and lets his hooves smack against the hard wood of the stall door.

Bang!

"Hey, did you hear that?"

"I think there's one over here."

Cupping his ears again, waiting. He knows the men are coming close. He can smell them and he can feel their eyes upon him now, watching through the slats of his stall.

"Getta load of the size of him!"

The voice does not belong to the man with the chains, but it makes no difference. He readies himself.

"He's a big'un all right."

A low whistle.

"I bet he was a looker in his day."

Ears flat back against his skull. Waiting, waiting.

"Not very pretty now. Take a look at those bones! He's starved near to death."

"Last legs, I'd say. Poor old fella."

The scrape of the bar being lifted; the creak of hinges.

He snorts, lowers his head, waiting. A new strength is pulsing though him. The fire in his legs doesn't matter at all.

"Hey there, big fella. How ya doin'?"

It is dark inside the stall but he can see the shape of a man coming forward, hand outstretched.

"Hey, there, boy."

Waiting, waiting until the man is close enough.

"Hey, old boy."

Rearing back with all his might. Head up, hooves ready to strike.

"Look out!"

"Get back!"

The door slams shut—just in time.

Hooves striking wood, a hammer blow. Splinters flying into the air.

Bang! Bang!

"You okay?"

"That was close!"

Rising up again for another strike as the metal bar scrapes back into place.

Bang! Bang!

Bang! Bang!

"Whew, what a nutcase!"

"Wonder how long he's been in there?"

"Take a look at that stall. Filthy. I'd be a nutcase too."

He waits now, head low. The air is hard to breathe. The pain is white-hot. But he won't give in.

The men are stupid enough to make another attempt. They click their tongues and talk in soft voices.

He feels only contempt. How can the men think they can trick him with their soft ways? Soft ways to hide the meanness, the need to hurt.

Bang! Bang!

"I think we're gonna need extra hands."

"Yeah, I think you're right."

His whole body is on fire now, flickering, trembling. Still he kicks and kicks and keeps on kicking. Long after the voices fade away. Long after the screaming of the mares stops and the only sound is the rain, gentle now against the tin roof.

Bang! Bang! Bang! Bang!

Morning light is creeping, dull and gray, outside the barn. It pokes through the wooden slats and falls in faint bars across the dirt floor.

Bang! Bang!

Still he kicks and kicks and keeps on kicking. It's all he can do. Because he cannot run.

Shiloh

Brrrr—

In the shadowy dark the sound is cut off before it has any chance to bloom. Before it has any chance to wake up the old couple sleeping down the hall.

The girl does not say a word as she picks up the receiver and holds it to her ear. Not like she used to, like a dumb baby.

Hello?

And then repeating it. Like a dumb baby.

Hello?

Hello?

Hello?

The first time, years ago, there'd been a click in the middle of the train of wobbly hellos. The sound of dead air. Her own dumb baby voice.

Hello?

Hello?

Hello?

There'd been the tears she couldn't stop.

Hello? Is that you? I know it's you. When are you coming back for me?

There'd been only the dial tone. Nothing else.

And so she learned from then on to be silent. She learned not to cry. She learned to pick up the phone at the first sound and put it to her ear and just listen.

Silence.

That's all. But it makes no difference.

The call is what matters. The person on the other end is what matters, and the day of the year. The one day of the entire year the call will come.

Of course the girl never knows the time. It could be morning or afternoon or night. (Although more often it is night, when other people might be in bed.) Even so, she has to always be on guard, listening, waiting. She always has to be the first one to the phone.

This isn't always possible, in all the different places she's lived over the past few years. One place didn't even have a phone, it was such a dump.

But this place does. The phone is in the kitchen and

the old people are down the hall and anyway they sleep soundly through the night. And so when the call finally comes the girl puts the phone to her ear and listens and hardly breathes.

Sometimes if she listens hard enough she can hear a hint of something. The rustle of clothes or the clink of ice cubes in a glass. The sizzle of fire and ash.

Tonight when she closes her eyes she can smell cigarettes, even though the old couple doesn't smoke. She can smell perfume, like candy. Sweet.

When she closes her eyes and smells the perfume and the smoke she can wait. And wait. She can wait forever if she has to, although she hopes she doesn't have to. She hopes one day, if she's quiet enough, there will be a voice on the other end. But for now this is enough.

The girl waits and listens.

Maybe she can hear another sound now. Wet and soft. Steady. Rain? Is it raining there, too?

How far away does her mom live from the old couple's house? How far as the crow flies? Because that's what people say when they mean a place is closer than it seems. As the crow flies.

"W–w–wh–wh–wh . . ."

All at once the noise explodes out of the silence and the girl nearly drops the phone she is so surprised.

"W–w–wh–wh–wh . . ."

Like a siren, a police car coming closer and closer.

The girl knows all about police cars and ambulances. But this sound, it isn't a siren. This sound is human.

"W–w–w–whaaaaa! Whaaaaaaa!"

Somebody is crying.

Not the girl of course. She never cries anymore.

Somebody is crying on the other end of the phone.

"Shhhh–shhhhh–shhhh."

And somebody is trying to shush the crying, stop it before it grows louder.

"Shhh–shhh–shhh."

Getting more desperate.

"Sh–sh–sh–shhhhh."

Somehow the girl knows the "sh-shhing" isn't going to work. She can tell the baby—because that's what it is—the baby is going to rev itself up instead of down, even with the "shhhh–shhh–shhhh"s. The girl has heard enough babies crying in the places she's been. She's met enough people who must have thought they wanted a baby but didn't when they found out how much trouble they are. When the babies cry and cry and won't stop crying.

"Shhhh! Shhhhhh!"

"Whaaaaaa–whaaaaaa!"

When babies cry like that in the places she has been, people usually tell them to shut up.

"Meet your sister."

The girl clutches the phone closer. Her heart nearly stops dead in her chest.

"A screamer."

The voice is exactly how she remembers. Low and gravelly. From the cigarettes.

"Just like you."

The girl opens her mouth. Is she supposed to talk now? Is she supposed to answer back? What does her mom want her to do?

"Happy Birthday, Shy."

Click.

And it's over. Just like that.

One click, and the sound of her mom's voice and the siren cry of the baby (*a sister, she has a sister!*) are gone.

Click.

Like they were never there at all.

Jessalynn

Brrrrnnnnnnng!

The sound comes from nowhere and everywhere.

Brrrrnnnnnng!

The woman tries to ignore the sound. She tries to stay in the cozy dark and hold on. To where she is. To the bundle in her arms. But she can't.

Brrrrnnnnnng!

The sound is already reaching through the darkness, hooking her like a fish and yanking her upward, arms empty.

"Hello? Hello! Jess! Hey, girl, wake up! Jess! Wake up!"

The woman recognizes the voice. Too loud for this time of night—or morning. Is it morning already?

"Jessalynn DiLima! Haul it outta bed, girl! E-mer-gen-cy. I'll be there in thirty."

Click.

Ah, now the woman can return to the dark. Sink back into darkness. Ignore the doorbell when it rings.

E-mer-gen-cy.

Eyes open. Just a squint, but open.

E-mer-gen-cy.

The curtain edge holds the barest hint of light. Rain pattering against the glass, soft and low. A vague memory of something harder, of thunder and lightning deep in the night.

The woman squints at the bright red numbers hovering on the bedside table. Morning, for sure. Way too early.

"I'm going to kill you, Nita."

The old redbone hound dog draped at the woman's feet lifts her head, thumps her long tail once.

"It's okay, Bella. You don't have to get up."

The dark wet eyes have a guilty look. Or maybe the woman is just imagining it. Not so long ago the dog would have been up like a shot, ready for anything. But now there's a dusting of white along her muzzle. The dog's head drops back onto the faded quilt.

The woman sits up and swings her legs over the edge of the bed. She stretches her arms into the air.

"Ahhh!"

A spasm of pain.

Slowly, carefully this time, she tries again, stretching, rising to her feet. Gently she kneads her thumbs into the small of her back.

Mornings mean stiffness now. Stiffness means she's getting old.

"Too old for e-mer-gen-cies. At four thirty in the morning," she grumbles, but of course there's no one to hear. The dog, Bella, has already gone back to chasing rabbits in her dreams.

For fun. For inspiration. For you.
Atheneum.

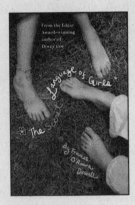

The Secret Language of Girls
by Frances O'Roark Dowell

Kira-Kira
by Cynthia Kadohata

The Higher Power of Lucky
by Susan Patron

Beneath My Mother's Feet
by Amjed Qamar

Standing for Socks
by Elissa Brent Weissman

Here's How I See It—
Here's How It Is
by Heather Henson

Atheneum Books for Young Readers ✴ *Published by Simon & Schuster*

what if no one could hear you?
would they think you had nothing to say?

Melody has a photographic memory. She remembers every word that is spoken around her and every fact she has ever learned. Melody also has cerebral palsy, and is entirely unable to communicate. It's enough to make a girl go out of her mind.

Then she discovers a computerized talking device that will allow her to communicate for the first time ever. It's a dream come true! But what if her teachers, her classmates, her friends don't want to hear what Melody has to say? What will become of her dreams? What will become of her life?

From award-winning author **Sharon M. Draper** comes a book as heartbreaking as it is hopeful, about a girl you'll never forget.

From Atheneum Books for Young Readers
Published by Simon & Schuster
KIDS.SimonandSchuster.com

The story of a group of kids,
with no musical talent whatsoever,
who form a rock band and find out
that EVERYONE can get by with
a little help from their friends.

And visit zebrafish.com to find out how *you*
can make a difference, as well as play games,
watch webisodes, and read about the band
members while *you're* there.

From Atheneum Books for Young Readers
Published by Simon & Schuster
KIDS.SimonandSchuster.com